"If there was ever an indulged, pampered, worship-the-ground-he-walks-on male, it's you!"

"But of course." Her outburst had not even dented his infuriating self-assurance.

"Let me tell you—"

But it was as far as she got; lifting his hand, Alex very slowly brushed across her lower lip with the back of one finger. It was the gentlest of caresses, yet it silenced her more effectively than any blow would have done.

"Be quiet—you talk too much. Your lips—" the softest of butterfly touches once more "—were not made for talking."

REBECCA KING lives with her husband, two daughters and the latest in a long line of much-loved hamsters in an old redbrick house in a village in Worcestershire. She has always wanted to be a writer, and worked as a journalist and wrote children's stories before moving on to her favorite field—romance fiction. Researching locations for her books is the ideal excuse for her main interest—travel—and she unwinds by watching old black-and-white movies, especially John Wayne Westerns.

Books by Rebecca King

HARLEQUIN PRESENTS
1477—DARK GUARDIAN
1638—LETHAL ATTRACTION

Don't miss any of our special offers. Write to us at the following address for information on our newest releases.

Harlequin Reader Service
U.S.: 3010 Walden Ave., P.O. Box 1325, Buffalo, NY 14269
Canadian: P.O. Box 609, Fort Erie, Ont. L2A 5X3

REBECCA KING

Vendetta Bride

Harlequin Books

TORONTO • NEW YORK • LONDON
AMSTERDAM • PARIS • SYDNEY • HAMBURG
STOCKHOLM • ATHENS • TOKYO • MILAN
MADRID • WARSAW • BUDAPEST • AUCKLAND

For my editor, Luigi
for his help with the Italian in this book—and
much more besides

ISBN 0-373-11678-0

VENDETTA BRIDE

CHAPTER ONE

'NOT Alex Baresi!' Lori, her sea-green eyes darkening in horrified disbelief, leapt to her feet. 'He isn't coming here, is he?'

'Now, now, my pet, don't get in a state.' Reaching across, her father patted her slim hands, which were clenched so tightly that the knuckles showed white. 'Of course he is. After all,' he went on soothingly, 'he's head of the family firm now, so he'll naturally——'

'Head of the jackal pack, you mean.' Lori's lips twisted bitterly. 'How stupid of me. He certainly won't want to miss out on being in at the kill, will he? Not when he's spent the last four years bringing us to our knees.'

'It's all my fault.' Her father ran his fingers through his grey, thinning hair and Lori looked down at him, seeing with a heart-wrenching pang the lines of worry etched deep into his once youthful face. 'Nearly two hundred years of Paget Crystal, and I've let it come to this.'

'No, Dad, you mustn't blame yourself!' she exclaimed hotly, and felt the old familiar guilt spiralling inside her. 'If only I hadn't persuaded you to send me out to Venice, I'd never have met Alex and none of this would have happened.'

Her voice choked into silence and, swinging abruptly on her heel, she went across to stand looking out at the rolling lawns, not quite so perfectly manicured as they had once been.

That fateful summer... Between school and art college, her father had wanted to send her to summer school in Italy to study Venetian glass-making techniques, but she, an only child, cosseted and protected by him since the early death of her mother, and fresh from the sheltered convent school, had instead begged to stay within the security of a family. Her father had recently got to know Alessandro Baresi, Senior, at a trade fair so it had seemed ideal for her to stay with them. The Baresi family... In spite of her inner turmoil, she smiled at the memory of their warmth and Latin exuberance. Of course, Alex hadn't been there, not at first...

'Nonsense.' Behind her, her father's voice cut through images of the past. 'The Baresis have been expanding their empire for years.'

She turned slowly back. 'Yes, I suppose you're right. And we're just the latest company for them to get their predatory claws into.'

'And anyway, I've told you, just because you and Alex didn't hit it off, that has nothing to do with it.'

Not hit it off. That's one way of putting it, Lori thought ironically, although of course she'd never been able to bring herself to tell her father the whole pathetic little story of why Alex and she had quarrelled. And yet, surely, *surely*, just because four years ago, as a young, inexperienced seventeen-year-old, she'd clumsily repulsed his sexual advances, could that really be sufficient reason for him to have pursued a private vendetta against her father's firm with such terrifying single-mindedness?

Yes, it could, she thought with sudden conviction, and a shiver ran through her. The main memory of Alex Baresi that had haunted her by day and often by night over the past four years was of his chilling ruthlessness, and his ice-cold anger when he was thwarted in anything he wanted. She'd been afraid of him then, and that fear, she knew with awful clarity, was still slumbering somewhere not very far beneath the surface.

'I'm sorry, Dad, but I can't meet him. After all——' she forced a smile to try and soften her words '—you'll want to keep things civilised, I imagine, and I just couldn't promise not to set about him and start scratching his eyes out.' Such beautiful eyes they'd been, pale, opalescent grey... 'What time's he coming?'

'I've arranged—or rather,' her father amended ruefully, 'when he rang me from the airport he informed me that he'll be here at three. He suggested—and I agreed—that it would be better to meet here at Mallards, rather than at the factory—a little more informal, and besides I don't want to alarm the work-force until it's all settled.'

'But——' She bit hard on her lip. It was futile to protest that Alex Baresi should not be allowed to pollute this lovely living-room of theirs with his presence. It would only upset her father even more, and besides, she thought helplessly, if Alex had announced his intention of coming here, then come he would.

Maybe—and with the thought icy fingers seemed to brush against her heart—maybe he was planning on casting his coldly acquisitive eye over this beautiful home of theirs. After all, it was part of the Paget Crystal property, since her father had been forced to remortgage it two years ago; so, as a clause in the take-over package, he might be intending—— Lori swallowed hard and closed her mind to what Alex might be intending.

'I really do think you should be here,' her father remonstrated, though still mildly. 'After all, as my only child and the heiress to Paget's——'

'If only I'd been a boy,' she broke in fiercely. 'We two together could have fought him off.'

'My dear child——' her father took her hand '—I wouldn't want anything different. You know you're the pride of my life.' And Lori felt the intense love and loyalty surge through her. 'But this sorry business will affect you at least as much as it does me and, when I rang James, he agreed. He'll be here, of course, to check the fine print on our behalf—and not only as our chief accountant.'

He gave her a teasing smile and Lori's eyes blurred as she looked down at the neat hoop of diamonds on her left hand. Dear James, so dependable, so loyal—he'd certainly fight their corner.

'Bye, Dad.' She gave him a quick hug. 'I must go. I've told Bob I'll let him have the preliminary sketches for that new range of vases by tomorrow, and I still haven't finished them.'

'You promise you'll get back for the meeting?' Her father's voice pursued her.

'I'll do my best.' And with a smile and a wave she was gone.

Lori roared through the arched gateway in the high red-brick wall, scarcely seeing, so familiar had they been since baby days, the words 'Paget Glassworks 1874' picked out in darker brick. She turned automatically to park in the chairman's space, then braked hard. Another car was there already, a dark blue Rover. She scowled at it resentfully, but then gave a faint sigh. Just another sign of the times. In the old days, no one would have dared—or wanted, for that matter—to park there, in her father's spot.

She swung in alongside, the nose of her Mini almost grazing the other car's bumper and, snatching up her shoulder-bag, got out, slamming the door.

A flight of outside stone steps led up to a landing from which opened a line of offices and the small room she used as her design studio, but for a few moments she lingered in the cobbled yard. This was the original end of the glassworks, where, in 1797, Ephraim Paget, her great—and a half a dozen more greats—grandfather had set up his tiny glassblowing business. When she was little, she'd never tired of hearing the story.

'Did he really—*really* walk all the way from Liverpool without any shoes when he was only thirteen?'

She'd asked her father the question a hundred times, and, 'Yes, he did, my pet,' he'd solemnly assured her, 'every step of the way—with only dry bread to eat.' And the five-year-old Lori's eyes would fill with tears.

Now, Ephraim, along with twenty other Pagets, stared down from the panelled walls of the boardroom, for all the world as plump and prosperous-looking in the Lawrence portrait as though he'd been born with a dozen silver spoons in his mouth and hadn't the faintest idea what it felt like to walk his feet to pulp.

The lump, which had been in her throat for days, swelled suddenly, painfully. 'Oh, Ephraim,' she whispered under her breath, 'you must have been so proud of this place. I hope your ghost isn't around to see what's happening.'

She gave a little sigh, then straightened her slim shoulders resolutely and walked on up the steps.

As she passed her father's office she glanced at the door and saw, through the frosted glass, a shape. Mrs Johnson, her father's secretary, but no—it was a bulkier, unmistakably male outline. Of course—James, doing some last-minute preparation before the meeting.

Lori opened the door, her mouth lifting already in a warm smile. But then, as the smile froze, her hand flew to her mouth and she stared blankly across the room.

The man, his back half turned to her, was lounging back in the black leather swivel chair, his long legs stretched out in front of him, his feet propped casually on the desk, studying a document. He had taken off the jacket of his pale grey suit—it was slung carelessly across the desk—loosened his tie and undone the top button of his white shirt.

Without glancing up, he said, 'Ah, good. Put it here,' and jabbed a tanned finger imperiously at the desk.

Lori's first instinct was to turn tail and flee, but then the righteous anger took over. Taking a deep breath, as much to steady the sudden treacherous weakness in her body as to control that anger, she closed the door with a click and advanced into the room.

'I said, put it here.' This time the barely veiled impatience crackled in his voice.

She stood looking down at him. The haughty, aristocratic features, the thin lips, only the fuller lower one marring the perfect features and hinting at the sensuality which she knew all too well lay beneath the chill, forbidding exterior... Jet-black hair, swept back, except for one lock which fell forward over the tanned brow, imparting a totally deceptive air of vulnerability. As did the thick, stubby black lashes, that without warning lifted to reveal a pair of opal-grey eyes—which were now subjecting her to a coolly dispassionate regard.

Just for a second something seemed to flicker in the chill depths of those eyes, but then whatever it was had gone and Alex Baresi was getting to his feet with the lazy grace which she remembered so well.

'Lorina, what a pleasant surprise.' The blatant irony in his tone grated on her and when he held out a hand she ignored it.

'H-how dare you?' She glowered at him but heard the tremor in her voice, and knew that it was born less of her still simmering anger than of the old fear of this man which, long buried, was even now spurting through her. 'Get out of here!'

With a toss of her long, pale blonde hair, she pointed dramatically to the door.

But he merely shook his head sadly. 'You know, *cara*, you have not improved in the slightest—at least——' he paused and allowed his gaze to rake over her body in a deliberately provocative regard which instantly peeled away the security of her turquoise linen dress and left her naked '—not in your manners.'

At her sides her hands clenched together until the nails bit into her palms, but all she allowed herself to say tautly was, 'You don't realise, I'm sure, that this is my father's office, and that is his chair.'

'Really?' And with studied insolence he dropped back into it.

Tears of impotent fury stung her eyes. 'Get out of that chair, and out of this room! You—you don't own Paget Crystal yet.'

'No,' he agreed smoothly. Shooting back his cuff, he glanced at the slim gold watch at his wrist. 'I have another forty minutes to wait for that pleasure.'

As she stared down at him there was a tentative knock at the door and before she could react he called peremptorily, 'Come.'

The door opened and Mrs Johnson appeared, pink and flustered, clutching a sheaf of computer print-outs.

'The papers you wanted, Mr Baresi. Oh, hello, Lori, I—I didn't know you were here.'

Lori's throat tightened. Her father's devoted secretary for over twenty years, and already selling out to the enemy. How could she? Their eyes met and the pink in the older woman's cheeks darkened to dull red. As she placed the papers on the desk, to be rewarded with a grunt of thanks from Alex, she shot the girl a look of mute appeal.

'Don't worry, Mrs Johnson.' Lori laid a hand on her arm. 'I understand.' All too clearly, she thought bitterly. If Alex Baresi demanded something and was denied it, few people would be strong enough to withstand the whirlwind of his anger.

As the door closed, she swung round again to face him, but he was engrossed in the print-out, running a long finger down the columns of figures, his black brows contracted in a frown. She edged nearer so as to look over his shoulder, then sucked in her breath in outrage.

'What have you got there?'

'Your current sales figures, of course.' He did not even deign to look up.

'Give them to me.'

She reached over and made a grab for the papers, but he was too quick for her. Even as she caught hold of them his fingers closed over her wrist and, as she struggled to free herself, his grip tightened. He said not a word, only turned his head slightly and looked up at her, but at the expression in his grey eyes her fingers went limp and she let the papers fall back on to the desk. She glowered down at him, rubbing fiercely at her tingling wrist.

'You've got no right to look at those. They're confidential.'

'For the next——' he gave another swift glance at his watch '—thirty-two minutes, perhaps. But they will have to be disclosed then, and I merely believe in going into any business meeting adequately prepared. In this particular case, of course,' he went on with a thin smile which reached nowhere near his eyes, 'I needed to ensure that I was presented with the actual figures and not some imaginary ones, carefully doctored to deceive an innocent buyer.'

'You—innocent!' she burst out, swelling with indignation on behalf of James, honest to the nth degree. 'You—you're just playing your sneaky, underhand tricks to the last.'

A flush of anger flared on his hard-edged cheekbones. 'I trust, *cara*, that you, of all people, are not intending to lecture me on honesty in business matters.'

'And what's that supposed to mean?'

'Merely that Baresi International may play hard but— unlike some other companies in the market place—we invariably play straight.'

'Straight for the jugular, you mean, don't you?'

'If necessary, yes,' he agreed coldly. 'After all, it's the most efficient way I've found yet of finishing off a creature that's halfway dead already.' He turned back to the print-out. 'These figures are quite appalling. Even more disastrous than I'd been led to believe.'

'And whose fault is that?' Her voice shook. 'You're the one who's been waging a cold-blooded vendetta against us.'

'Vendetta?' He raised one quizzical eyebrow. 'A trifle melodramatic, surely?'

'I don't think so. After all, since when did any Italian—and least of all a Baresi—choose to forget, or forgive, an insult?'

'True. Some things, certainly, are never forgotten.' Just for a moment, their eyes met; then, as the quick blush rose in her face, her lashes flickered and fell.

'But even so, what has that got to do with the sad demise of Paget Crystal?' he asked.

'Everything, of course. Every move we've made these last four years you've damn well been there, cutting the ground from under our feet. We were on the point of signing a contract with that international hotel chain—until you moved in at the last minute, behind our backs, with a counterbid we couldn't hope to match. The talks we were having to provide all the glassware for that luxury cruise liner—the deal you offered them, I still don't see how you made a penny out of it.'

'I assure you, Lori,' he cut in suavely, 'I have never made an agreement yet where Baresi did not come out on top.'

'No, I can believe that, at least,' she agreed bitterly. 'And then, with our share price plummeting to rock bottom, you buying them up—through an intermediary, of course, so that, at first, we didn't even know where the attack was coming from, although we should have guessed. And now you're all set to take us over completely.'

'Take you over? Providing you with a rescue package is how I would put it—throwing you a lifeline.'

Lori laughed mirthlessly. 'Oh, yes, you drive us on to the rocks, knock the planks from under us and then talk graciously about throwing us a lifeline. Just how hypocritical can you get?'

'That's enough!'

Terrified by the sudden flare of anger in Alex's pale eyes, Lori tried to back away, but with one fluid movement he was on his feet again and was swinging her around to face him.

'L-let me——' But the rest of her furious words were swallowed up as his mouth came down hard on hers. Desperately, she tried to clamp her lips and teeth against this invasion of her body. But he forced her head back until a soft moan of protest was wrenched from her throat and then, as her lips parted slightly, he thrust in his tongue to plunder her mouth.

Her eyes spitting impotent green fire at him, she hung helplessly in his arms, until gradually she felt herself filled with the taste of his mouth, the smell of his body, warm, and wholly, totally male. And, in an instant, she was back in the garden of that Venetian villa, the night breeze sighing softly in the cypress trees and in the distance the shouts and laughter from the terrace where she and the Baresi family had all been enjoying her farewell party.

Down here, though, there were only the two of them; he, in casual light-blue cords and a white shirt—open-necked, as now—she in her best white sleeveless poplin dress. As they strolled, he paused to pick a couple of sweet-scented pink roses and solemnly tucked them into her hair. She smiled, wide-eyed and a little uncertainly, up at him, then he casually slipped an arm around her shoulder.

She stiffened momentarily, but then relaxed against him. Alex, at twenty-seven, was light years older than she, heir-apparent to the Baresi empire and playboy *extraordinaire*; his lifestyle was a constant source of rich pickings for the gossip columnists and the *paparazzi*. And yet with her, he'd consistently behaved as though he were no more than an indulgent older brother...

The path ended at a circular marble pool with water-lilies and fish, flickers of silver in the moonlight. She sat down on the edge, letting her fingers trail where a little stream from the hills above the villa trickled into it. When a fish swam slowly up and gently nibbled her little finger she turned to Alex, smiling.

His face was a pale blur above the even paler blur of his shirt, but there was something in the intent way he was watching her which all at once made her stomach lurch and her throat contract so that she could scarcely breathe. Putting up his hand, he lifted a few strands of silky ash-blonde hair, almost white in the moonlight.

'You know, Lorina, with those wide, sea-green eyes and those flowers in your hair, you look just like Botticelli's *Primavera*, the very spirit of spring.'

His voice sounded oddly tight and as she stared up at him, her lips parted, he let her hair drop to her shoulders; then, taking her by the elbows, he drew her to her feet and kissed her. At first, the kiss was gentle, even ten-tative, but then, too surprised to respond in any way, she stood frozen in his arms; the kiss hardened and—as now—his tongue thrust past her lips and teeth so that the wine on his breath mingled with the honeyed sweetness of her mouth as he ravaged it.

One hand came up to cup her breast and, very deep within her, Lori felt strange, wholly new sensations stirring. She wanted to resist but her limbs were heavy, rooting her to the ground. But then, with an incoherent mutter, he slid his hand to the small of her back, pulling her against him; she felt his body quicken, and the sudden shock of that hard, uncompromising masculine pressure set every alarm bell in her brain clamouring wildly.

'No!' With a violent shudder of distaste she brought her arms down, breaking his grip.

As she stumbled back from him, all her sexual immaturity laid bare like a raw wound, her hand instinctively flew up to deliver a flat-handed slap across his cheek. It landed with a sound like a rifle shot, then there was silence. But, not daring to wait for any reaction, she turned and, sobbing for breath, ran headlong back up the path to the villa.

The rest of the family had seemed not to notice when she reappeared, pale and over-wrought; or when Alex, set-faced, also returned, though the puffy imprint of her fingers on his cheek was there for all to see. Only Giulia, one of Alex's cousins, a silent, intense girl whom Lori had had very little to do with, had, under the pretext of passing her a dish of olives, given her hand a sympathetic squeeze...

That last time, it was she who had broken free. Now, though, as suddenly as he had taken hold of her, Alex released her and she staggered back, fetching up hard against her father's desk.

'H-how dare you? You—you swine!' she gasped and, glaring at him through a fringe of dishevelled hair, wiped the back of her hand fiercely across her mouth, not once but several times. But the gesture was futile bravado, for she knew with sick certainty that, as on the last occasion, Alex Baresi's kiss would linger in all her senses for weeks—no, months—to come.

'You know, *cara*——' his lips twisted into a thin, contemptuous sneer '—you still kiss like someone who's never been kissed in her life before. So chaste, so— adolescent.'

She winced under the gibe but then, still struggling for composure, said coldly, 'If we're trading insults, it's pretty adolescent, isn't it, that just because Alessandro Baresi, the great lover, has his male pride dented when he fails to seduce a naïve little seventeen-year-old——'

'Seduce! You flatter yourself, my sweet. If I had seriously set out to seduce you——' his voice flicked lazily around her '—do you really believe that you could have held out against me?'

Lori gasped in outrage. Of all the arrogant, insolent, macho—Italian swine! And yet—and yet, through her anger, she could feel emanating from him, twining itself round her to subdue her, what four years previously she had just dimly sensed and fled from. Now, though, she could recognise it for what it was—the highly dangerous sexual allure of the predatory male animal.

As though for reassurance, she clutched the fingers of her left hand and twisted agitatedly at her ring.

'You wouldn't dare speak to me like that if James were here,' she flung at him.

'James?' His voice exuded boredom.

'Yes. Our chief accountant—and my fiancé,' she added defiantly.

'Your fiancé!'

For the first time in their exchange he looked, if it was not an impossibility, momentarily off-balance. But before she could draw back, he had taken hold of her slim hand and lifted it to examine the dainty circlet of diamonds.

'Very chaste, very pure, very—appropriate.' His voice mocked her. 'My congratulations. I hope that you'll make each other very—happy.'

'I'm sure we'll do our best,' she replied woodenly, and snatched away her hand, all too aware though of the faint warmth from his fingers which lingered on her skin.

'And now, if you'll excuse me, Signor Baresi, I have work to do—some designs I need to complete.'

'Your own?'

Was she imagining it, or had the temperature in the room suddenly dropped by twenty degrees?

'My own?' She looked blankly at him. 'Of course they are.'

'Not more pickings from industrial espionage, then?' he asked silkily.

'Industrial espionage?' She seemed capable of nothing but parroting his words.

'Let me put it in language you will no doubt understand. Are they your own designs—or more that you have stolen?'

CHAPTER TWO

'STOLEN!' Lori gaped at Alex. 'Of course they're not stolen. I've never stolen a design in my life—or anything else, for that matter,' she added fiercely.

'No?' This time there was no pretence whatsoever at civility —just cold, contemptuous disbelief.

'No, I damn well haven't!'

'Oh, come now, Lorina. That wide-eyed innocence— it might have had me fooled once, but we both know better now, don't we?'

'Just for the record——' she stood in front of him, her backbone steely with angry pride '—what am I supposed to have stolen?'

'Just for the record,' he mimicked her cruelly, 'my prototype designs for the Geneva exhibition, of course.'

'The ones you told me about when you showed me around your studio on Murano, you mean?' she replied slowly, trying to assimilate his words. 'But I never saw them. When I asked, you wouldn't even let me look at them—you said they were top-secret.'

'Precisely.' His lips twisted savagely. 'And so, when I was called away and was foolish enough to leave you there alone, you somehow opened the locked safe and helped yourself to them.'

'No!' Shaking her head against the miasma of bewilderment, she edged away from him to put the desk between them, pressing her palms hard down as if to seek reassurance from its solidity. She closed her eyes for a split second. Perhaps everything of the last four years—Signor Alessandro Baresi's death, opening the way for his son's ruthless vendetta against them, Alex's reappearance today, and now this dreadful accusation which was making her feel quite sick—was a horrible nightmare.

But when she opened her eyes again, the nightmare had not gone away. It was standing there; flesh and blood, clothed in immaculate Italian tailoring, with eyes like chips of ice, watching her across her father's desk.

'No, Alex, you're wrong,' she said unsteadily, for somewhere among all the bewilderment was pain that he should believe this of her. In her urgent desire to make him understand, she came back around the desk and put her hand on his arm. He glanced down at it expressionlessly, then brushed it off as though it were an insect. She bit her lip, but forced herself to go on.

'You did give me some of your designs, but—but you must remember, you said you'd finished with them—that they were discontinued lines.'

Her mouth tightened against the pain of unwanted images. That last afternoon, before her farewell party—Alex, still the indulgent older brother, teasing her, rumpling her hair, casually taking up a sheaf of designs.

'Here,' he'd said offhandedly, 'take these home with you—a souvenir of me.' She'd watched breathlessly as he'd signed the top one in his bold, flowing hand—Alessandro Baresi—then handed them to her with a funny little sidelong smile. And because she was a fair way to hero-worshipping this overwhelmingly handsome young man, she'd hugged them to her, too overcome to speak...

'Those designs,' she said now, 'they were beautiful. When I got home and showed them to my father——'

'Ah, yes, your father. I trust that he rewarded you adequately. After all, he must have been well satisfied with your month's work.'

She felt, all at once, as though he had kicked her viciously in the solar-plexus. 'Are you seriously suggesting that my father sent me out to stay with your family simply to see what I could steal?'

He nodded grimly. 'I couldn't have put it more clearly myself.'

Two bright petals of colour blazed in her cheeks. 'You haven't even met my father. If you had, you'd know that, whatever you might think of me, he's absolutely incapable of a dishonest action.'

His thin lip curled. 'How touching—the loving daughter leaping to the defence of her innocent father.'

'Yes—innocent! I don't know what crazy idea your twisted mind has got hold of, but to think anything else of him—or me—oh, it's just too ridiculous.'

'Is it? Who better-equipped than you for such a role? Brought up since birth in the world of glass-making, and yet so young, so naïve and so—inexperienced.' He smiled, not pleasantly. 'I've even asked myself, many times since, whether your outraged reaction that night in the garden was not all part of a carefully calculated act. Yet now, I can see that in this, at least, I was mistaken. You were sexually unawakened then, and you remain so now. Despite the best efforts, no doubt, of this fiancé of yours.'

Her green eyes blazed into angry life. 'You know nothing about James, so leave him out of this.'

'Gladly.'

From her whirling mind a thought crystallised itself. 'So this vendetta of yours——' his brows came down in a thunderous scowl but she hurried on '—it's had nothing to do with—with the way I reacted that night?'

He looked genuinely astonished. 'My dear Lorina, you flatter yourself. Do you seriously believe that I should have devoted the last four years of my life to avenging such a petty affair? I assure you,' he added, with a light, careless cruelty which cut her to the bone, 'it was forgotten within the hour.'

'But what on earth makes you think that I took those designs?'

'The indisputable fact that within a remarkably short space of time from your return home, my prototypes— with the most minor of amendments—appeared under the Paget label.'

Lori drew a deep, shuddering breath. She hated— loathed this man with every fibre of her being, but somehow she had to get through to him. 'Look, Alex, all the designs I brought back with me, the ones you *gave* me——'

'Plus a few more.'

'*No*!' In her frustration, she banged one fist into her palm. 'I left them here when I went off to college. It's true my father admired them so much that he said he'd like to adapt some for our own lines, but only after I'd assured him over and over that everything you'd given me was finished with as far as you were concerned. You must believe me.'

But his only response was a cynical laugh. 'A pretty story. Such a pity that it's a pack of lies. It was sheer coincidence, of course, that the only designs you used were those prototypes. The rest, no doubt, were consigned to the company's trash can!'

'No, you're wrong. I've——' But she bit back the words. Her pride wouldn't give him the chance of yet another cruel put-down by telling him that, when she'd come home after her first term at college, she'd retrieved all the designs her father had not used and even now they were hidden away in a drawer of her dressing-table.

Another thought struck her. 'If you really believed that we'd done this, why didn't you sue us for breach of copyright? Surely the Alex Baresi we all know and hate would have had us in court in double-quick time.'

'That was my first reaction, of course,' he agreed suavely, 'to take you and your precious father for every last penny you possessed. But then I decided to give myself the even greater pleasure of seeing Paget Crystal slowly bleed to death.' As she stared at him, horrified, his voice dropped to a tiger's purr, as though he were savouring every word. 'Yes, Lorina—death by a thousand cuts. So much more pleasurable in every way, don't you agree?'

The hairs on her nape stirred at the cruel slant of those thin, beautifully moulded patrician lips. 'You—you devil!' But her mouth was dry with fear, and the words came out as an uncertain whisper. 'Aren't you afraid that, one dark night, someone will sneak up on you and slide a stiletto blade between your ribs?'

He gave a careless shrug. 'I sleep well at nights, I assure you. But now——' he glanced once more at his watch '—it's time to go. I'm sure you'd hate to keep your father waiting.'

'I'm not coming to the meeting,' she said quickly.

He frowned. 'But surely, as one who so clearly has the best interests of Paget Crystal at heart——' stonily, she ignored the biting sarcasm '—you will want to play a full and active part in the final negotiations.'

'Negotiations!' she exclaimed hotly. 'You—negotiate? Don't make me laugh. You—you're like some damned highwayman who pulls up alongside a stage-coach, cuts free the horses, shoots the coachman through the heart, holds a pistol to the passenger's head and then says, "Right, now let's negotiate." '

Alex laughed lightly. 'How very perceptive of you—and flattering.' He clicked his tongue in mock reproof. 'But flattery, my dear Lorina, will not make me change my mind. And——' all at once his voice hardened '—I wish you to be there. So—come.'

Swiftly, he knotted his tie and slipped on his jacket, then opened his executive case and slid the sheaf of print-outs into it. Straightening up, he placed a hand on her arm, and when she hesitated the outspread fingers tight-ened momentarily, pressing just a little into the soft flesh of her inner arm. She glanced up sharply, reading the warning in the grey eyes, and in the warm, still air of the office she shivered. Then, tight-lipped, she allowed herself to be led outside and down the steps.

In the car park she said stiffly, 'Can I give you a lift?'

'No, thank you. I have a hire car.'

He gestured towards the blue Rover and Lori's lips tightened. Of course, she should have guessed. None of her father's employees would have dreamed of using his space—only this arrogant, smooth-as-silk swine.

'But if you will be so good as to lead the way,' he went on, seemingly oblivious to her thoughts, 'I'll follow.'

Without another word, Lori swung on her heel, got into her Mini, reversed hard and shot out of the car park, almost under the wheels of a Paget delivery van. She raced away, deliberately taking every narrow, twisting back street of the small town. But all the time her rear mirror was filled with a sleek blue bonnet, and when she roared up the winding drive to Mallards to draw up at the porticoed entrance in a spurt of gravel the Rover glided in alongside her.

Alex climbed out and stood looking up at the lovely old house, its mellow stone façade half obscured by the branching yellow sprays of the huge Mermaid rose.

'Sizing up your latest acquisition?' The unwise words spilled out before she could hold them back.

He eyed her coldly for a moment, but only said, 'It is a beautiful house.'

'And is, as you are no doubt fully aware, part of the Paget company assets since my father was forced to re-mortgage it. He's lived here since he was a child, and he and my mother lived here before she...' Her voice trailed away. This house, where she too had lived all her life and had spent such an idyllic childhood, until that happiness was blighted by her mother's early death.

'Look, Alex,' she went on, the words suddenly tumbling out, 'whatever you think we—my father and I—have done, please don't turn him out of here. He loves this place. It—it would nearly kill him to have to leave it.'

She looked up at him, her full lips parted tremulously, her sea-green eyes shimmering with unshed tears. But he merely quirked one sardonic eyebrow.

'Appealing to my better nature, Lorina? But surely you know I haven't any?'

And with an enigmatic smile he turned and led the way up the steps and into the spacious entrance hall. A low murmur of voices came from a room to their left and, as they entered, three dark-suited men, who were standing in a little huddle by the marble fireplace, swung round to face them.

'Ah, Lori.' With a relieved smile, her father detached himself and came towards them. 'Signor Baresi.' He held out his hand to Alex and she felt a surge of pride; whatever his private anguish, he had schooled himself, as always, to show nothing but perfect politeness. 'You know my daughter, of course. May I introduce Frank Simpson, our company lawyer, and James Forsyth, our chief accountant?'

Alex favoured the two men with one brief nod between them.

'I was sorry to hear about your father,' Mr Paget went on. 'I admired him very much.'

Alex inclined his head slightly once again. 'Thank you. I remember you wrote to that effect at the time.'

Lori, standing between the two men while these stilted courtesies were exchanged, could not hold herself back any longer.

'Dad, he thinks we——'

'Perhaps we could make a start,' Alex's suave voice cut in, 'I think we're a moment or two late already.'

He turned towards the oval rosewood table so that Lori could do nothing but slide quickly into a chair between her father and James. Too late, she realised that this manoeuvre brought her directly opposite Alex, who, despite being on alien territory, outnumbered by four to one, proceeded effortlessly to take charge of the meeting.

Constantly, as the discussion proceeded, she felt her gaze being drawn unwillingly across the highly polished table. She studied him covertly from beneath her lashes as he dealt incisively with a series of legal points raised by Frank Simpson. What a smooth devil he was. A handsome devil, with those dark Italianate looks—she couldn't deny that—but a devil through and through, as proud, and as lethal, as Lucifer, the Lord of Darkness himself.

And to have made an enemy of this man... Icy little fingers ran up and down her spine. But how on earth had she got hold of those designs? Instead of being in that locked safe, where he thought they were, they must somehow have been mixed up with the ones he'd so casually given her, without even looking through them. Yes, that must be it. All this dreadful business was his own careless fault, but—she glanced up again and one glimpse of those hard-planed, unyielding features was enough to tell her—she'd never in a million years be able to convince him of that.

Having successfully countered the last of Frank's objections, he leaned back suddenly in his chair, stretched out his long legs under the table and came into sharp contact with hers. As he looked at her directly for the first time in the entire meeting, Lori felt herself colour deeply, then she jerked back her legs, tucking them safely under her chair.

Mercifully, at that moment, James embarked on a last-ditch attempt to achieve the most favourable financial terms, and that disconcerting gaze was withdrawn as Alex proceeded to demolish his arguments with quite unnecessary venom. Lori tried to catch James's eye to give him a commiserating smile, but he was glaring across the table, his fair hair dishevelled, his normally rosy face pale. Poor James—he was an experienced, highly trained accountant, but one would as soon put a woolly month-old lamb in the arena with a raging tiger as expect him to stand up to the appalling Baresi.

'Now, gentlemen—and, of course, Miss Paget——' a graceful nod '—I think we've reached a position where I can sum up what has been agreed to date. Just the salient points, of course—my lawyers will draw up the final contract for our joint signatures. Essentially, Paget

Crystal is to become a subsidiary company of Baresi International from July the first next. Paget will continue trading under its existing name and, in the foreseeable future, I guarantee that all its employees will retain their positions.'

Lori gave her father's arm a squeeze. His eloquent plea on behalf of the work-force, some of whom had been with him for forty years or more, had at least achieved one small victory.

'This concession,' Alex's smooth tones continued, 'will not of course apply at management level. I intend to draft my own nominees in all key positions, with one exception.' He turned to Lori's father. 'If you wish, I am prepared for you to remain on the board as a consultant.'

'Consultant! Baresi puppet, more like!' Lori, barely aware of her father's restraining hand on her arm, almost bounced out of her seat in sudden fury. 'Pick Dad's brains, don't be so stupid as to throw away a lifetime's priceless experience in glassmaking, but make sure all the key decisions from now on are made at the centre of the spider's web in Venice.'

She broke off, her breast heaving, bracing herself for the next thunderbolt from Alex. But he was sitting quite still, watching her over his steepled fingers. A totally new expression lay in those grey eyes; though it was quite unreadable, it none the less sent a peculiarly intense feeling of unease through her, although she could not have said exactly why.

'Well, Mr Paget,' he said at last, as though her outburst had never happened, 'do you agree?'

Lori, out of the corner of her eye, saw her father, after a second's hesitation, nod a brief acceptance, and she clamped her teeth together on the anger which still boiled inside her.

Alex nodded in return. 'But, in all other areas, personnel will be replaced.' He paused, then went on silkily, 'The entire design team, for example.'

'What—all of us!' The shocked exclamation was torn from her.

'Naturally.' His eyes dared her to protest further.

'But that's just not fair. Sack me, if you want to— and yes, of course, I should have guessed this was coming,' she added bitterly. 'Your day just wouldn't be complete without it, would it? But the rest of them— they had nothing to do with——'

'Signor Baresi,' her father broke in, 'I really must advise you to reconsider. You are proposing to break up an outstanding design team. Lori herself is a brilliant young——'

As Alex's lips twisted in a totally humourless smile, Lori cut in desperately. 'No, Dad, there's no point in arguing with him. And in any case, the way things are going, I wouldn't want to stay anyway. But to sack Bob and the others, that—that's diabolical.'

Her cheeks flushed with anger, her green eyes stormy with passion, she tossed back her long blonde hair and glowered across at him, to be met by that inscrutable, wholly disconcerting look once more.

'Purely as a matter of interest——' James leaned forward, his voice crackling with hostility '—I assume that this clean sweep of yours also applies to the accounting department.'

Alex gave a negligent shrug. 'To the chief accountant, certainly.'

Lori, certain that his eyes were still on her, kept her head lowered. Something else to blame herself for. If only she hadn't let slip the fact that she and James were engaged. For it was this, she felt certain, which had damned him to be swept up in Alex's ruthless quest for vengeance as surely as if he had Paget blood in his veins.

'There are two final points I require to be added to the draft agreement,' Alex continued. 'Firstly, although this house is now Baresi property, I have no objection to you, sir——' he inclined his head to Mr Paget '—residing here for your lifetime, or for as long as you wish.'

Lori, with a little sigh of heartfelt gratitude, glanced up quickly, but he was not looking at her now. So, in the end, through some strange quirk of compassion, he'd stayed his hand from that final execution. And really, in other ways, something had been salvaged from the wreckage. At least her father remained on the board, and the Paget name would continue—in her mind she saw for a moment all those comfortable-looking Pagets whose portraits lined the boardroom wall... James, like herself, would not have stayed on anyway, and with his qualifications would have no problem getting another job. And Bob and the rest of the design team—well, there had been several attempts recently by rival firms to lure them away. They'd only stayed on out of loyalty to her father. Yes, one way and another, things could have been a lot worse...

'Just one last point.' Her eyes flew to Alex once more. There was something—*something*—in his cool, controlled voice which made her know with sick certainty that he had saved until last one final dreadful ace which he was about to bring into play.

'And I should perhaps make it clear that all of the foregoing is dependent on this factor.' He paused fractionally but, while the men only stared at him in puzzlement, Lori, her nerves drawn out so fine that they were almost snapping, could not contain herself any longer.

'And what is this factor?'

'That you, Miss Paget, agree to be my wife.'

CHAPTER THREE

'YOUR wife!' Lori repeated stupidly, then, as the full import of Alex's words finally penetrated her numb brain, she felt the colour drain from her face. 'You mean—*marry you*?'

He nodded. Dimly, she heard the shocked exclamations around her, the angry protests from the other three men, but her eyes were locked with Alex's.

'B-but that's impossible,' she stammered. 'You're playing some kind of stupid joke on us—on me.' For that would be quite in his nature—a cruel practical joke. But he looked across at her, no hint of amusement in his flint-grey eyes; a gleam of malicious pleasure perhaps, but no laughter.

'It's no joke, I assure you, Lorina.'

She wanted to leap to her feet, bang the table and shout. Of course I won't, damn you! But her entire body was trembling violently and she was transfixed in her seat.

'But—but why?'

He lifted one shoulder in an elegant half-shrug. 'Let us just say that I have a fancy to marry, while you—you are the heiress to a company which is about to join the Baresi empire. In the circumstances, what could be more fitting?'

'But that's like some feudal wedding contract—an arranged marriage to cement two kingdoms together.' She stared at him, her eyes black with shock, the rest of her face paper-white. 'It's—it's hideous. A horrible idea.'

33

'In that case——' an air of infinite regret infused his voice '—I shall be forced to withdraw my offer.'

'Well, that's just fine by me.' Dimly, Lori heard someone's voice beside her, then an arm went round her. She swung her heard sharply, so dazed that, for a moment, she could barely recognise her father. His fingers tightened comfortingly on her shoulder. 'Don't worry, pet. I won't allow this to happen.'

But she turned back to Alex. 'Let's just get this absolutely clear, shall we? Either I agree to your proposition or the whole deal is off.'

'How very quick you are today, Lorina.'

'I see,' she said slowly.

'But you can't even consider it for a moment, Lori,' put in her father urgently. 'Frank, using such a threat—it can't possibly be legal, can it?'

The lawyer pursed his lips. 'It's highly unusual, and morally indefensible, of course. But there can be no objection in law if——' a swift glance at Lori '—both parties are in agreement.'

'Well——' her father breathed a sigh of relief '—there's no problem, then. As Lori clearly is not willing to——'

'Wait a minute, Dad. I must have time to think. Paget's——'

'No, Lori. If the company's survival is dependent on this, well, it must go to the wall. I'm sorry, Signor Baresi,' he looked directly across at Alex, his voice all at once stiff and formal, 'but there can be no question of my daughter—my only daughter——' she felt his fingers tighten on her shoulder again '—sacrificing herself in this way. All other considerations apart, you are presumably unaware that she is already engaged to be married.'

Oh, he knows, he knows all right, thought Lori, with a savage twist of bitterness. But that just adds to his enjoyment, doesn't it? James... In the turmoil of the last few minutes she'd almost forgotten his existence. Her eyes went to him now, and she saw that he was leaning back in his chair, his face very pale, his mouth set.

'James.' It was an appeal, through quivering lips, but he met it with the faintest of shrugs—a shrug which said clearly, There's nothing I can do, darling. It's your decision.

Just for a moment she thought of pistols at dawn, and had the image of James utterly destroying this man then turning to take her in his arms. But then, shoulders bowed, she turned her head away, gently disengaging herself from her father, and looked back at Alex.

'But—why?' she repeated. 'Why are you trying to do this?'

'I've told you—it's a fitting arrangement. And besides——' his voice dropped, so that no one else could catch his words ' —we have some unfinished business, you and I.'

'Oh.' The rosy tide of colour surged into her cheeks, half-anger, half-shame at the memories his words evoked.

The others had faded into the background now. They were mere spectators of the drama being unfolded between her and the man seated opposite, casually flicking his gold fountain pen against a folder, watching her as though he were some ruthless predator confronting a mesmerised rabbit. He was so casual, so unutterably sure of himself. Damn him! She felt the fierce tide of anger sweep through her, then ebb away, leaving her icy cold.

'Just supposing I should, for some reason, dare to turn down this "proposal",' she spat out the word, 'is there no other offer we can make?'

'But you have nothing else *to* offer.'

She winced at the contempt in his voice. It was true, of course—she felt the sick certainty creep through her. She knew, from anguished late-night discussions with her father, that there was no other rescuer in sight; Alex Baresi had seen to that. And now, having brought the company to the brink of ruin, he was all too clearly prepared to administer the *coup de grâce* if he did not win the battle of wills that was being waged, in this oh, so civilised drawing-room, across the gleaming rosewood table.

'Of course,' Alex went on casually, 'it is still not too late if I should decide, after all, to sue for breach of copy——'

'No!' Her father, strained almost beyond bearing, should not have to meet this further blow—at least, not yet. 'Please, no,' she added huskily, the appeal shimmering in her eyes.

'So, it's agreed, then?' he said, as though he were sewing up any ordinary business deal.

'No, Lori, I absolutely forbid you——'

But she waved her father to silence. 'Please, Dad, don't. I'm of age—in fact, in just a few weeks I'll be twenty-one—and I can make up my own mind.'

Despite her firm words, the tight little knot of misery which had formed itself in her stomach was beginning to spread rapidly through the rest of her body. To try and quell it, she turned to Alex with one final appeal. 'There's nothing else you will accept?'

When, almost imperceptibly, he shook his head, she whispered, 'Very well, I agree.'

Just for a moment, she thought that she had glimpsed—what? A spark of triumph?—no, something more than that in his inscrutable grey eyes. But it was so fleeting that she knew she had imagined it.

With a swift glance at his watch, Alex returned his attention to the three men, who were all sitting as though turned to stone. 'In that case, gentlemen, as soon as the necessary paperwork has been completed, the documents can be signed.'

'But, Signor Baresi——' her father had found his voice again '—if you really are intent on marrying my daughter, there are arrangements to be made, although I feel, in the circumstances, that in any case a long engagement will be preferable.'

Lori, locked into her private world of misery, felt a tiny flicker of hope warm her. A long engagement—yes, surely that would give Alex time to reconsider his crazy off-the-cuff decision—or even give someone somewhere the chance to realise that his life just wasn't complete without taking over Paget Crystal?

'I'm sorry.' She roused to hear Alex speaking with a finality which instantly snuffed out the little candle-flame of hope. 'I fly back to Italy in two days' time, and I wish Lorina to accompany me in order to prepare for our wedding.'

As Lori gaped at him, too crushed for a reaction of any kind, she became aware that James was slowly getting to his feet.

'If you'll allow me, sir,' he addressed her father, totally ignoring Alex, 'I'd like a few minutes with Lori—alone.'

'No, James.' She turned agonised eyes to him. 'Don't try to make me change my mind.'

He continued, though, to look questioningly at Mr Paget.

'Of course.' But Lori squirmed with shame to see that her father had glanced first at Alex, as though seeking permission, and only when the latter spread his hands in an elegantly dismissive gesture did her father speak.

'All right.' She was barely audible. 'Let's go into the garden, shall we?'

Standing up, she leaned her hands on the table for a moment for support, then led the way out through the french windows and across the terrace. She walked faster and faster, as if to shake off the dreadful scene in the house, heading automatically towards the rose bower, her favourite part of the garden.

As James followed, more slowly, she ran like a wild thing down the crazy paving steps, under the rustic archway smothered in the pink-pearl blooms of New Dawn, and came to a standstill beneath a pergola heavy with the creamy-white flowers of Alberic Barbier and the beautiful coppery peach of Albertine, which filled the afternoon air with their luscious perfume.

But Lori stared unseeingly around, her eyes hot and gritty. This lovely place had always been a refuge from reality. But not today...

When James appeared, she was pacing up and down, her arms wrapped tightly round herself as though the warm summer afternoon had turned suddenly to mid-winter, her feet crushing the faded petals which lay thick as wedding confetti on the grass.

She swung around to face him, her face set. 'Please, James, I know how you must be feeling, but don't try to talk me out of this. I have it in my power to keep Paget's going, and to let Dad spend the rest of his life here, so I must go through with it.'

Her voice trembled, and when he did not speak she went up to him and put her hands on his chest, as if for reassurance. 'You must see, I—I've got no choice. All of this, it's my fault. Oh, I've done nothing wrong,' she went on hastily, as James stared at her, 'but it's because of me that Alex has been behaving the way he has. And now I've got the chance to put it right.'

'Oh, my poor darling!' He kissed her brow lightly, then pulled a rueful face. 'You're quite right, of course. In the great scheme of things, Paget's is more important than any of us.'

She gave a small murmur of assent. Even while she agreed, though, she could not prevent the treacherous little rush of disappointment that James was not prepared to fight like a raging bull to keep her.

His face hardened. 'God, what a foul swine he is!'

Lori felt the tears rising in her, a flood tide which if it began to flow would never be quenched. For James's sake, she mustn't cry.

'Hey, watch it.' She gave a ghostly smile. 'That's my fiancé you're talking about.' But at the gallows humour, her voice cracked and broke.

'Oh, Lori, don't.' He took her awkwardly in his arms and held her to him, then spoke into her hair. 'Anyway, we're not finished yet. I was doing some hard thinking back there, and I reckon that there's still a way for us to get the better of him.'

Of Alex Baresi—surely not? Surely, no one would ever—could ever—get the better of him? 'But you saw the way he was. Whatever we offer him, he'll never give up Paget's now.'

James laughed grimly. 'I agree that he gives every sign of being the kind of bastard who, once he's got his claws around something, you have to damn nearly hack them off, one by one, before he'll let go. But——' he hesitated before going on, his voice all-at-once constrained '—if you can go along with what I suggest, well, before too long he'll be more than happy to be rid of Paget's—and you.'

She pulled herself free, to gaze at him blankly. 'What do you mean?'

'I'm saying, go ahead with this charade of a marriage, but keep it just that—an empty charade. Look,' he went on, a note of irritation entering his voice, 'divorce still isn't all that easy in Italy, but even there one of the surest ways to get a marriage annulled is on the grounds of non-consumption. Do you get what I mean?' as she still looked at him in bewilderment. 'Keep the bastard out of your bed!'

Lori's green eyes almost swallowed the rest of her face. Until now, her mind had been in such a turmoil that she hadn't looked any further than the actual ceremony. Now, though——

'But—but will he let me?'

'I think so. Baresi is a ruthless swine, but he's an arrogant one too, and I can't see him demeaning himself by taking any woman by force, not even an uncooperative wife.'

'No, I suppose not,' she agreed slowly, at the same time shuttering her mind against the terrifying images his words were conjuring up.

'What's more, he's the kind of dynastic-minded swine who'll be wanting lots of little Baresis running around in double-quick time. So, if you're not prepared to provide them, well——' He shrugged meaningfully. 'And this way, our marriage will just have been postponed for a while, and you'll still have saved yourself for me.'

He grinned at her triumphantly and she forced a smile in return. And yet . . . a niggle of doubt remained. Could she really stand up against Alex's undoubted reaction

when she confronted him with the reality of their marriage? And besides, James, this is me! she wanted to cry
out. It's my body that you're talking about, as if it's
just a pawn in a game.

She looked uncertainly at him. This was a totally new
James; she'd never seen him like this before. True, he
was always so cool, so level-headed, seeing his way
through with unflappable clarity, to the centre of any
problem. But he was speaking now with such a chilling
brutality that, if it had been anyone but him, it would
have repelled her.

'So—it's down to you, darling. If you can hold out
against him—and that shouldn't be too difficult, feeling
the way you do about the swine—I reckon he'll be more
than happy to get shot of you.'

'Yes, but he'll still own Paget's.'

'If I read him right, he'll hate the name of Paget's
nearly as much as he hates you!'

Deliberately to set out to arouse the hatred of Alex
Baresi—she'd had a sample of that already! Lori's mouth
went dry with stark terror at the mere thought.

'I reckon he'll be glad to accept a company buy-out
and be rid of the lot of you. So——' he held her away
from him by the elbows, smiling confidently at her
'—you can do this, darling, can't you? For us?'

And when she thought of Alex, and of this final humiliation he was inflicting on them both in his relentless
pursuit of revenge, all her doubts were swept aside in a
wave of love and loyalty.

'Yes, I can, James. Of course I can.' And, throwing
her arms around him, she kissed him.

'What a touching scene.'

The coolly ironic voice made her leap back as though
she were still a gauche teenager. Furious with herself,

she swung around and glowered at the newcomer. 'What do you want?'

Alex raised one dark eyebrow at her tone. 'A word with you,' he said coldly. 'So, if you'll excuse us——'

He glanced pointedly at James, who glared back at him. The mutual antagonism between the two men crackled in the air but it was James who dropped his eyes and backed off.

'Well, Lori——' James gave her hand a squeeze '—I'll be off now.'

'Oh, must you, darling?' She shot the other man a defiant look. 'Do stay to dinner, won't you?'

'Perhaps I should tell you, Lorina,' Alex put in silkily, 'your father has very kindly invited *me* to dinner.'

Of course—she should have guessed that her father would insist on doing the correct thing by inviting his prospective son-in-law, however much it stuck in his throat.

'Thanks, Lori,' James spoke directly to her, 'but I'm sure you'll understand if I don't. Bye.' And he was gone.

She watched him until he disappeared around the shrub border, then turned slowly to face Alex. Here, under the rose-wreathed pergola, his jet-black hair was brushed by the lowermost branches, and his features were cast into a deep shadow against the early evening sun. He had taken off his tie again and undone the top couple of buttons of his shirt, and she could see a few tiny whorls of crisp hair, black against his tanned chest, while higher up, just at the base of his throat, a tiny pulse was beating.

She stared, fascinated, at that pulse, and felt her own begin to beat in time with it, measured and regular... She swallowed, then wrenched her eyes away.

'So, you're quite determined to force me to go through with this travesty of a marriage?' Somehow, she managed to make her voice offhand as though she were commenting on the weather.

'I'm not "forcing" you to go through with anything.' Alex, leaning nonchalantly against the pergola, watched her.

'Not forcing me? Don't give me that rubbish!' she snapped. 'It's coercion—blackmail of the most blatant, wicked kind.'

'If you say so,' he replied blandly.

He was still watching her, something in his regard making her think suddenly of a cat which, replete from having feasted on small birds all day long, would see a sparrow hop just within range, and is unable to resist the impulse to lift a languid paw—and kill. That enigmatic stare terrified her, but she had to fight back or be left crushed and bleeding—just another Baresi victim.

'You know something?' she hurled at him. 'I loathe you, despise you!'

He lifted one shoulder by a millimetre. 'I can live with it.'

'Yes, well, I don't suppose I'm the first woman to say that.'

He appeared to give the idea serious thought, then said, 'I don't suppose you are.'

Lori stared at him, her fingers plucking at her skirt, her nervous tension and anger effervescing inside her. 'Haven't you shamed me enough—accusing me of being a thief, firing me in front of the others—without forcing this final humiliation on me?'

He looked pained. 'A humiliation to marry Alex Baresi? There are many women, *cara*——'

'And don't call me *cara*. I'm not your darling, and I
never will——'

'—in Italy—and elsewhere—who would not agree with
you.'

'That's a matter of opinion,' she said sullenly.

'No, *cara*, it is a matter of fact.'

He was so damn sure of himself! Somehow, she was
going to get a reaction from him—whatever that reaction might be. 'You said, back there, that marrying
me would set the seal on your take-over——'

'Not quite so crudely as that, I'm sure.'

'But I seem to remember that the Ancient Romans,
whenever they took over a new province, would let the
soldiers loose to rape the local women. I'm amazed you
don't just rape me and have done with it. After all, you
tried hard enough last time!'

His light laugh grated on her. 'Oh, Lorina, what a
vivid imagination you have.'

'But why not settle for that?' she persisted. 'Why
bother with marriage—surely you've got your revenge
without that?'

'Revenge, hmmm?' He regarded her thoughtfully.
'Perhaps, because I think that my revenge will be all the
sweeter this way. And more long drawn-out.'

'And that really is all that it is for you, isn't it—
revenge?'

Another shrug. 'If you choose to think so. But I
promise you, *amore mio*,' he paused fractionally, and
now his voice fell to a purr, 'that, in this case, revenge
will be at least as sweet for the vanquished as for the
conqueror.'

Lori's heart skittered wildly with alarm. 'I...' she
began, and then her voice died absolutely.

She swallowed, running the tip of her tongue nervously along her upper lip, and tried again. 'And anyway, you didn't have to treat James like that. He knew nothing about this business with the designs.'

'Ah, yes, the inestimable Mr Forsyth.' He spoke the name as though it were an unpleasant smell in his aristocratic nostrils. 'Believe me, I'm doing you a favour.'

'A favour? And just how do you make that out?'

'By rescuing you from a marriage with that desiccated adding-machine. A man like that, he would never have made you—happy.'

The blatant innuendo in his voice made the colour storm into her cheeks. 'And you imagine you can, I suppose?'

Her unwise words merely provoked a lazy smile. 'I don't imagine: I know it.'

Straightening up, he sauntered slowly across to her while she, as though mesmerised, stood rooted to the spot. He looked down at her, a faintly wry smile on his lips. 'You know, Lorina, you intrigued me four years ago, and you still intrigue me now. There is something about you—that cool blonde hair; those pale green eyes which darken so when you are angry; that slender, graceful body, which still retains the slight awkwardness of youth; and that air of slight aloofness.' He could have been talking to himself. 'They all send out "keep your distance" signals to any man who strays too near. And yet, underneath, I sense other far more powerful signals—hidden fires.'

'Oh, how ridiculous——'

'Signals of which the worthy James is completely unaware—and from which he would have run a mile if he had ever so much as suspected their existence.'

'You're wrong, quite wrong,' she began in a shaken voice. 'James is——'

'—a cypher, a nothing man. Look at the way,' he rode through her protests, 'he has given you up without a struggle. A real man would kill to keep a woman like you.'

She flinched at the contempt in his voice. Of course, she'd had the same disloyal thought herself. But it was simply that James, in the final analysis, was cleverer than the oh, so clever Alex Baresi. And that was a thought she would have to cling on to through the weeks and months ahead.

'Tell me,' she went on with an effort at icy disdain, 'when did you first think of this horrible idea? Has it always been part of your vendetta—the final act?'

'No, it was not in my mind at all—until today.'

So sudden? The speed with which he worked was frightening. 'But supposing you change your mind tomorrow?'

'I don't think so. I've always found that my most successful decisions have been made without forethought.'

'Yes, but that's in business.'

'Is there any difference? I act as my instincts tell me, and they are telling me now, that you and I——' He left the sentence unfinished, but his slow regard, just as in the office, seemed to strip her clothes from her, leaving her body exposed, as though not just his eyes but his fingertips were tracing a lazy trail over every inch of her quivering flesh.

Beside them was a Fantin Latour rose. He snapped one of the deliciously scented pink flowers and, as she stood motionless, tucked it into her hair. It was a re-run of that scene in the villa garden and, caught up in a time warp, she could only stare blindly up at him.

There was a strange, unreadable expression in his grey eyes. 'You know, my sweet, at the villa four years ago——' she gave a little start—so he, too, was recalling that evening '—I told you that you were like Botticelli's *Primavera*; a young girl, barely formed, the very spirit of spring. But now you are like summer—awakening, ripening, ready to bloom.'

He was so near to her that his breath stirred the fine blonde wisps of hair at her temples and, in spite of all her hostility and anger, she felt a shaft of fear go through her as the full consciousness of his sexual allure pierced her. Oh, it was quite unconscious—not forced or practised in front of the mirror every morning, but worn as an integral part of him, like a second skin—and therefore infinitely more lethal.

She could stand up to him, of course. For James's sake, she could do anything. But even so, she took a step away from him now, her hand going up to her mouth in a nervous gesture.

'Ah, that reminds me.'

As she went to jerk back even further, he caught hold of her hand; then, before she could protest, he had dragged the diamond ring off her finger. She suppressed a little gasp of pain as it grazed the knuckle; then the pain changed to horror as—after looking down at it for a moment—he tossed it into the air for it to plop neatly into the small stone pool in the centre of the rose garden.

'What the hell did you do that for?' Her voice rose in outrage.

'James can retrieve it later if he wishes.'

'But you should have let me give it back to him,' she said mutinously.

'Should I?' Alex was supremely unconcerned.

As she watched, he pulled off the signet ring from the little finger of his right hand. 'I have not, of course, chosen your engagement ring yet, but until then——' and he slid it, still warm from his skin, slowly down on to her fourth finger. She gazed down at it, her heart beating wildly, strange emotions churning inside her. It was a wide band of gold, set with a disc of dark green jade, and it was very heavy. To Lori, it felt like the first link in a metal chain to bind her to him.

'It—it's too big. I'll lose it,' she said jerkily, but when she made to pull it off, his fingers tightened over her hand.

'No, you will not.' Over their clasped hands their eyes were inches apart, and her eyelashes fluttered and fell.

'Th-the coat of arms—what is it?'

'Two lions—one the lion of Venice; the other the Baresi lion.'

She looked down at the two rampant creatures facing one another, frozen snarls on their jade faces. It was as if Alex had put his personal brand on her, for wearing this ring made her feel like a Baresi possession as nothing else could have done today.

'You will wear this until I give you a more suitable one. It was presented to a Baresi by the Doge of Venice in the sixteenth century, for services rendered.'

'Conveniently getting rid of one of his enemies, no doubt?' she said waspishly.

But Alex merely laughed. 'Oh, something more commendable than that; my ancestor was, so I'm told, his favourite mistress and exceptionally well-versed in the arts of love.'

Still holding her hand between both of his, he lifted it. His lips touched the back of her hand in a formal salute but then, instead of releasing it, he turned it over and softly kissed the palm. His lips were no more than brushing her warm skin, and yet, from that tiny area of flesh which was in contact with his mouth, she could feel the strangest sensation, as though tiny currents of electricity were prickling their way along every nerve-channel in her body, sending up little showers of sparks in her blood as they short-circuited wildly.

At last, after an endless lifetime, he raised his head and surveyed her flushed face, her parted lips. She saw his silver-grey eyes darken, then he permitted himself a small, secret smile.

That smile brought her sharply to her senses. Was she mad—forgetting already her promise to James? No, she wasn't. She jerked her hand away as a red tide of shame and anger flooded through her.

'I'm going in now.' But she sounded breathless, as though she'd been running all afternoon among the hills which sloped up gently behind Mallards. She paused, to give herself a chance to recover, then went on haughtily, 'I imagine my father will want to begin making arrange-ments—for the wedding.' Just to say the word made her mouth burn as though she'd swallowed acid.

'He will not have to concern himself with that,' Alex said firmly. 'My mother will wish to take it all upon herself.'

'But how can she?' A terrible thought shot into her mind. 'We *will* be married here, won't we?' she demanded.

He shook his head. 'I told you, we're going out to Venice in two days' time.'

'Yes, but I thought that was just to meet your family again.'

'No. My mother, I am sure, will wish us to marry in Venice.'

He took her hand again but she pulled herself free, glaring up at him. 'I don't want to be married in Venice. This is my home and I want to be married here. At least, I don't want to be married anywhere—not to you,' she shot him a killing glance, 'but if I've got to be married anywhere, it must be here—in the village church.'

The little church where she'd been christened, and where in all her girlhood dreams she'd seen herself coming down the aisle on her father's arm, all in white, with a veil, her eyes misty with happiness... The only thing which had steadfastly remained a blur was the face of the man waiting at the altar for her. Try as she might, she'd never been able to see his face. And even after they'd become engaged, it was somehow never James who'd turned and smiled and held out his hand to her...

'Lorina——' but for once there was no anger at her defiance in Alex's voice '—you will bear with me, please. It has always been my mother's wish that all her children—and especially, of course, her adored only son——' he gave a crooked smile, which she refused to respond to '—should marry in the church in Venice where she and my father were wed. You will make her very happy if you agree.'

His voice had lost all of its cool incisiveness, and there was a new, almost constrained note. 'You see, my parents' marriage was—what do you say?—made in heaven, and it will please her greatly, I know, to see us married in the church of Santa Maria dei Miracoli.'

Lori bit her lip. She'd been humiliated and manipulated all afternoon, and here was her chance to fight back... But Signora Baresi had been so kind to her that summer—so motherly that, for the first time, Lori had realised the enormity of her own loss. And she'd been very sad when her father had told her that Signor Baresi had died, for he'd been very kind to her also—an older version of his son, spoiling her, giving her a set of tiny glass animals which he himself had made when he was young.

'All right, I agree,' she said softly. But then, because she couldn't allow Alex to think that he had in some way subtly defeated her yet again, she added woodenly, 'After all, it doesn't really matter where we get married, does it? This is one marriage which, for sure, has not been "made in heaven".'

CHAPTER FOUR

As ALEX eased the sleek nose of the Alfa Romeo into the maelstrom of traffic outside Marco Polo airport, Lori continued to stare fixedly out of the passenger window. They had been met by a uniformed chauffeur—the same one, she'd realised, who'd met her here four years before—but Alex had, apparently on a whim, decided that he would drive, so they were in the front while Giovanni reclined at his ease in the back.

Alex had probably only done it to avoid conversation, for the speed and volume of the traffic would cut out all but the most perfunctory of remarks. She shot him a resentful glance but then decided, at the sight of that hard-edged profile, that she too preferred an almost silent drive.

She stared down at her hands, clasped tightly together in her lap. Her pink cotton skirt was creased. It always was after five minutes' wear, so what on earth had possessed her to choose it? Defiance, most likely. When he was leaving Mallards two days previously, Alex had said casually, 'By the way, don't bother bringing many clothes with you.' And when, prickling like a hedgehog, she'd asked coldly, 'Why not?' he'd replied, 'Because I shall be buying you a new wardrobe.'

New wardrobe, new life was the clear implication behind his words. 'And what about a wedding dress?' she'd enquired resentfully. 'No, don't tell me. I don't have any say in that either, do I?'

'For myself, I don't in the least care what you wear—
or do not wear—for the ceremony, but that too will be
taken care of.'

This particular piece of high-handedness had come as
a fitting conclusion to that appalling dinner with the three
of them spaced out around the enormous dining table.
Mercifully, the two men had carried the burden of the
conversation as she'd sat silent, making a pretence of
eating a little of the food which stuck desert-dry in her
throat, and distributing the rest in patterns around her
plate.

Gradually, with a sense of horrified betrayal, she'd
realised that her father, after his initial stiffness and re-
serve, actually seemed to be warming to Alex, falling
under his spell. Oh, Dad, how can you? she'd thought
bitterly. How can you be so gullible?

All too easily, she'd acknowledged seconds later.
Polite, charming and witty, Alex's conversation ranged
effortlessly from the latest scandals in Venetian politics
to the relative merits of the Italian and English national
soccer teams.

Was he doing it deliberately—setting out to ensnare
his future father-in-law? She studied him covertly, then
decided not—the charm, which could so easily dazzle,
was just an integral part of his persona. Once, she'd even
found herself smiling, then, as she sensed his eyes trav-
elling to her, had hastily replaced the smile with the
frozen indifference with which she was determined to
mask every emotion. And of course he could afford to
be smoothly affable, couldn't he? He'd won—he was
the victor, they the vanquished. The fact that he could
charm the birds out of the trees, as and when he chose,
just added to the bitter taste of defeat in her mouth.

Later, when he was leaving, as they'd stood in the open doorway, he had shaken hands with her father before taking her cold hand and kissing her cheek in a strangely formal gesture. Then, she and her father had stood watching in strained silence until the Rover was out of sight.

Mr Paget had cleared his throat, then said awkwardly, 'Alex—he's a good man, you know.'

'Is he?' Her voice had been drained of every shade of feeling.

Her father had turned to her. 'Lori——'

But she couldn't take any more, not tonight, so she had smiled with an empty vivacity and had said quickly, 'It's been quite a day. I'm off to bed.'

That had been the last time she'd seen Alex until they met in the departure lounge at Heathrow. Right at the last minute, just for a moment, she'd clung to her father as though she were still a child; but as his arms tightened around her, as if even then to prevent her leaving, she'd gently disengaged herself, that meaningless smile nailed into place.

'I'll see you again soon, Dad. Just as soon as we've fixed the date for the wedding.'

'Yes, of course.' Then he'd turned to Alex, who had been watching them both, a totally unreadable expression in his grey eyes, and had said gruffly, 'Look after her, won't you?'

And Alex had replied gravely, 'Of course.'

She'd said not a word as they were ushered to their seats in the first class section and, as the Alitalia jet began to roll, had deliberately closed her eyes to feign sleep. But then, as two sleepless nights took their toll, reality had taken over and she'd plunged headlong into a black pit of oblivion...

She registered that the car had swung inland away from the city and was running alongside a sluggishly flowing waterway. Suddenly, she was conscious of Giovanni, no doubt all eyes and ears behind them. She remembered from last time that his English was all but non-existent, but, even so, surely he would be picking up the vibes of tension zinging around them both?

Moistening her dry lips, she asked, 'Er—is that the Brenta Canal?'

When Alex nodded, she went on, her voice still very stilted, 'Are we going to your mother's villa, then?'

'Of course.' He, on the other hand, sounded completely relaxed. 'Why do you ask?'

'Oh—I just wondered.' She paused. 'W-will all the family be there?'

She felt him turn briefly to glance at her. 'Most of them. It's very short notice, of course, but my three sisters certainly will be. I gather they're all very anxious to renew acquaintance with their new sister-in-law.'

His sardonic tone was daring her to respond but, at the thought of the reception party awaiting her, all she could manage was a feeble, 'Yes, I suppose they are.' But then, because she had to know, she asked, 'Have you told them? About what I'm *supposed* to have done, I mean?' she added spikily.

'No, they do not know what you *have* done.' For Giovanni's benefit, no doubt, his voice sounded warmly affable. Only she would have caught the jagged edge of ice beneath. 'Like my father, I never mix business with family matters. They still think of you, *my sweet*,' and this time she winced inwardly at the barbed mockery, 'as that oh, so innocent seventeen-year-old who so entranced us all four years ago.'

'I see.'

Another long silence, then, 'I have my own house in Venice now, and we shall be married——' Lori's hands clenched convulsively '—from there. But it would not, of course, be proper for me to take you there now.'

'Not proper?' She swung around on him, only just fighting down the hysterical laughter.

'Something is the matter?' Alex, most of his attention on a teenager-crammed Fiat ahead of them, quirked a dark eyebrow.

'Should there be?' Lori's voice, under the impact of that cool eyebrow, rose sharply, then, remembering the 'eyes and ears' in the rear seat, went on in a hissing whisper, 'You do a ruthless demolition job on Paget's, fire me, *blackmail* me into a marriage when I'm engaged already——' her voice trembled at the memory of James's face that dreadful afternoon '—and then you have the nerve to talk about what's *proper*. You—you make me sick!' she wound up, between her teeth.

'So you have already told me,' Alex responded softly, 'and that makes us just about even, I should judge.'

'Oh, and how do you make that out?'

'Because thieves—especially thieves who look all innocent, all naïveté—sicken me also.'

'But I've *told* you . . .' she began, but then, clenching her hands together, she bit savagely on her inner lip to silence herself. Whatever it cost her, she would not demean herself any further by protesting her innocence yet again. He could believe what he wanted to—she couldn't care less what he or his precious family thought of her. And besides, the worse his opinion of her, the better. This way, in the end, he'd be all the happier to be rid of her, wouldn't he?

Alex swung the wheel and they turned into a gravelled drive which wound between an avenue of silvery hornbeams, then opened out to reveal a large but pretty stone house under a softly glowing geranium-pink tiled roof. It was built in an L-shape behind a formal garden, edged by low-growing lavender and rosemary hedges and narrow winding gravel paths, where several peacocks were strutting and flaunting themselves.

Just for a moment, Lori's fears and helpless anger evaporated and she took a long breath of sheer pleasure. In four years, she had forgotten just how enchanting this place was.

Giovanni, cramming his peaked cap over his iron-grey curls once more, was out of the car almost before it stopped. He opened her door but Lori, all at once quite incapable of moving, could only stare up at him, smiling palely. So, instead, he opened the boot-lid, snatched up a case in each hand, and disappeared in the direction of the pillared entrance.

Alex uncoiled himself in a more leisurely manner; he came around to her side and put a hand under her arm, so that somehow she was standing on the gravel, her legs trembling unsteadily beneath her. Without looking at him, she hitched up her shoulder-bag. He had not re-laxed his grip on her, and now it tightened. More bruises—she glanced down resentfully at the ring of pale blue finger-print shadows around her wrist from three days earlier.

'Could we dispense with the "Marie Antoinette before the guillotine act", do you think?' His voice, to an ob-server, would have sounded pleasant enough, but when she turned sharply to him his eyes were as warm as an Arctic sea. 'Or are you intending to sulk like this all the way down the aisle?'

'I'm not sulking,' she muttered.

'Really?' The polite enquiry jarred on her, like a wet finger across glass. 'But, in any case, you will be well-advised to remember that, for my family, ours is the romance of the century.'

'Oh?' She was stunned for a moment, then found a tart tongue. 'And just what makes them think that?'

He gave her a thin smile. 'Love at first sight, *amore mio*—or rather, second sight, four years on. I meet the young duckling who's turned into a beautiful swan and—love blossoms.'

She regarded him with hatred. 'What a cynical swine you——'

'However you feel about me personally, my sweet,' he cut in urbanely, 'you will remember that fact when you meet them.'

'Oh, of course. I'd hate to spoil their illusions.'

'Yes, I would hate you to.' His voice remained expressionless, but there was a warning glint in the grey eyes, a certain tightness of the thin lips which made her pulses pitter-pat with fear.

'Alex!'

The joyful exclamation made her jump and, swinging around, she saw Signora Baresi, her arms extended, framed in the doorway. A moment later, and Alex was clutched to his mother's plump bosom, lost in a torrent of unintelligible Italian. When he was finally released, she too was enfolded and kissed rapturously on both cheeks.

'Lori, my dear child——' Signora Baresi's English, like the rest of the family's, was almost as good as her son's '—I am so happy to see you here again.'

She took Lori's hand and patted it, then glanced down, clicking her tongue. 'Oh, that son of mine—always in such a hurry. He has not even bought you an engagement ring, so you have to wear his.'

'Yes, well, Mamma.' Alex's hand slid around Lori's waist and she went rigid as, unseen, his fingers dug into her side. 'As I told you on the phone, it was all so sudden. We set eyes on each other again—and that was it, wasn't it, *carina*?'

Agree—and quickly—his fingers said, digging in once more in that unsubtle warning. Lori wanted to jump up and down in rage and yell, so the whole villa could hear, This adorable son of yours, you may think the sun shines out of every one of his beautiful toenails, but he's nothing but a scheming, blackmailing *rat*!

But Signora Baresi's eyes were glistening with tears as she still held Lori's hand between hers, and she really couldn't bear to hurt her—at least, not today—so she forced the required brilliant smile into place.

The older woman held her now at arm's length. 'And you are even prettier than I remember.'

'But, Mamma, that's what love does for you!'

Swivelling round, Lori saw Alex's elder sister, Elena, smiling archly down at them from the entrance porch, and then, as the rest of the family cascaded down the steps she found herself engulfed in a torrent of laughter, tears, kisses and hugs. As she and Alex were finally borne into the villa, on a tidal wave of jubilation, she struggled desperately to keep a tiny private part of herself aloof. She knew, from four years back, just how easy it was to succumb to the Baresi family's infectiously exuberant charm; but she couldn't—mustn't, she thought despairingly.

'Giulia, my lamb, come and meet Lori again.' Signora Baresi was drawing forward Alex's cousin, who had been hovering in the background.

'Hello, Lori.' With a shy smile, the young woman kissed her on the cheek then took her hand, giving it that same secret, sympathetic squeeze which Lori remembered from that dreadful final evening four years ago. Don't worry, she seemed to be saying, I know it's nearly all too much for you, but I understand.

Lori gave her the first natural smile she'd managed in days and kissed her cold cheek in return. Perhaps this pale, reserved girl, of the family and yet somehow not wholly part of it—Lori recalled being told how, after both her parents had died, she'd been taken into the household, brought up with Alex's sisters and now worked in the design section of the Baresi glassworks—could be a friend, even some sort of ally, perhaps? She could never confide wholly in her, of course—Giulia was too much a Baresi for that—but, even so, any sympathetic companion in the weeks and months ahead of her was going to be something to be cherished...

'And now tea—real English tea.' Signora Baresi swept them through the delightfully cool house, shuttered against the late afternoon heat, and on into the courtyard garden beyond. Padded loungers and chairs had been set out in the shade of the trees, around a small pool where a worn stone cherub held a carved horn from which a fountain played.

Lori chose a small upright armchair—a lounger might make her lower her guard, and she mustn't do that, not for an instant. She set the chair down deliberately on the opposite side of the pool from where Alex was in lively conversation with Elena and her two teenage sons. The rapid to-and-fro of words and the flamboyant gestures—about, she gathered, how many goldfish there should be in the pool, and whether the local stray cat had helped himself to any—were like the final act of a

Verdi opera. Last time, these little dramas had privately amused her, and yet, at the same time, she had found it very pleasant—and had even sometimes thought wistfully how nice it would be to be part of such a lively, effervescent family...

Alex leaned forward, trailing a finger across the surface of the pool. A lock of black hair fell forward over his brow and he brushed it back. How good-looking he was—there was just no denying that. And more, much more than that—how sexy. Even in this completely relaxed family situation, he was exuding that aura of sexuality which he constantly carried around with him. He wore it as negligently as he did those casually elegant clothes... And how fortunate it was that she could recognise it, acknowledge it, even deep-down feel the faintest stirring of a response to it, yet be level-headed enough to know that sexual attraction—no, give it its proper name, lust—had nothing whatsoever to do with love... With James, she had so much more. The important things like love, affection, sharing...

'How rude we are, ignoring you, Lori.' Silvia, Alex's middle sister, broke into her thoughts. 'You will have to get Alex to teach you Italian—it's very easy, you know. And of course,' she darted Lori a teasing look, 'it's the language of love.'

'No, no, there won't be any need. I shan't——' Lori, caught off-guard, blurted out the words, then, colouring, pulled herself up hastily. 'I—I mean—I expect I'll soon pick it up just listening to you.'

She turned away and met Alex's grey eyes. There was an expression in them which, just for a moment, sent another of those *frissons* of fear up and down her spine. He couldn't know about the plot which James had hatched—could he? Sheer terror made her break out into a cold sweat. No, of course not. Even Alex's devious mind would not suspect that.

With careful casualness, she leaned forward and took one of the delicious little melt-in-the-mouth pastries that floated on cushions of rich cream. The look, though, which Alex had given her still hung oppressively on the air like a far-away thunder storm, and she was grateful when Marcello, the husband of Emma, Alex's youngest sister, only a couple of years older than herself, appeared in the doorway.

More introductions, this time formal, as Marcello had not been around four years ago, and then a nursemaid followed him out, carrying a miniature Marcello in her arms. Lori watched, smiling, as the baby was handed around for extravagant petting but then, as Emma went to drop the tiny scrap on to Lori's lap, she drew back in horrified alarm.

'Oh, no, please. I—I've never held a baby.'

There was a chorus of shocked exclamations, then the infant was dumped firmly on her knees, so that she was forced to take hold of him. He was so light, yet so solid, his black silky head propped against her arm, his plump sun-tanned legs kicking at the chair as he clutched at his beautiful dark-blue smocked romper-suit.

A very strange sensation began taking hold of her as she put out a tentative finger to stroke the tiny hand. Instantly it closed around her finger but, as she looked up smiling with delight, she met Alex's eyes again. They were quite unreadable, and yet there was something in them which once more set her pulses beating with alarm.

'He's the kind of dynastic-minded swine who'll be wanting lots of little Baresis running around in double-quick time.' As James's words leapt into her brain, she wrenched her eyes away, to hear Signora Baresi say comfortably, 'It is preparation for your own first baby—soon—*cara*.' As Lori gave a little gasp, she went on, 'Another Alessandro—that is what the whole family is waiting for.'

'Mamma, you are embarrassing Lori,' Alex cut in smoothly, but his eyes were still on her.

'Embarrassing her?' His mother looked astonished. 'By talking about *babies*?' But then her innate good manners stopped her saying any more, although her silence said louder than any words, *Dio mio*, these young English women, what do they think they are made for, if not to have babies?

Alex bent over Lori and lifted Marcello junior out of her arms. He held the baby, who squealed with joy, high above his head, then lowered him until the tiny hands could beat at Alex's face. Looking at him, Lori thought quite dispassionately, What a marvellous father he'll make. One day, perhaps, her cool inner voice reminded her, but they'll not be your children, will they? By then, you'll be away and married to James, laughing every day at the sweet revenge you've had...

Dinner, that evening, was out on the terrace beneath the vines which grew tangled with the white-starred jasmine whose perfume, released in the evening air, was intoxicatingly sweet. The meal was, if anything, even more fraught for Lori than that at Mallards. Sandwiched between Alex and his mother, as guest of honour—an honour she could well have done without—she had to endure a seemingly endless stream of good-natured banter, aimed, it was true, more at Alex than her, but which she too was forced to respond to, smiling until the muscles of her face ached.

By the time the leisurely meal was over and coffee had appeared, her nerves were screwed up so tightly that she would not have been surprised to hear them twang audibly like broken violin strings. Even though she had changed into a long-sleeved white lacy blouse to go with the pink skirt, each time Alex's arm brushed against hers her skin twitched like a cat's fur stroked the wrong way, and whenever his leg touched hers she jerked away.

Abruptly, she pushed away her half-empty coffee-cup and stood up. 'If you'll excuse me—I'm very tired.'

She did not look at Alex, but before she could move he was on his feet. 'I'll see you to your room.'

'Oh, no, really. I mean——' she began, but her feeble protest died away as he put a hand under her elbow and, to a chorus of '*Buona notte*, Lori,' she was firmly led indoors.

Once out of sight she tried to pull her arm clear, but his grip tightened. She swung round on him. 'I'm perfectly capable of finding my own way to my bedroom, thank you.'

'I'm sure you are, but you will please allow me to behave correctly. And *you* will continue to behave as the family expects.'

Somehow, Lori was up the stairs, along the wide corridor and outside her own door. Safety! But when she put her hand on the doorknob, Alex drew it away. He put both hands on her shoulders and she knew that he could feel the slight tremors which were running constantly through her entire body.

'You are trembling like a thoroughbred racehorse. Relax, *cara*.'

He smiled down at her, the easy smile of a man who was utterly sure of himself, and suddenly she was filled with the insane desire to leap at him, kicking and punching. Wisely, she did no such thing, but instead snarled, 'Relax? How the hell do you think I can relax?'

He nodded, as if in sympathy. 'Yes, I know that the days before the wedding can be very trying for all young women. The excitement, the anticipation——'

'It's not that, and you know damn well it isn't!' She stamped her foot in frustration. 'It's—well, why are you making me go through with this? After all, you admit that it's only for revenge. So, why can't we call it off? It's still not too late.'

'Of course it's too late,' he replied harshly. 'Everything is settled.'

'Maybe it is, but surely the great Alex Baresi can just as easily unsettle it?'

'I could do, yes,' he agreed evenly, 'but you see, *angelo mio*, just as I would never deny myself the pleasure of breaking in and schooling a wild young horse, I am now looking forward to taming a self-willed, spoilt young woman.'

His silky words sent the now familiar cold fingers of fear quick-stepping up her spine, but she tried to smother them in righteous indignation.

'*Spoilt?* Well, of all the nerve! Your mother and sisters, they all spoil *you* something rotten. If ever there was an indulged, pampered, worship-the-ground-he-treads-on male, it's you!'

'But of course.' Her outburst had not even dented his infuriating self-assurance. 'And as a good, docile little Italian wife, you will naturally be required to continue where they leave off.'

Lori swelled with outrage. 'Let me tell you——'

But it was as far as she got; lifting his hand, Alex very slowly brushed across her lower lip with the back of one finger. It was the gentlest of caresses, yet it silenced her more effectively than any blow would have done.

'Be quiet—you talk too much. Your lips——' the softest of butterfly touches once more '—were not made for talking.'

He bent his head, and almost imperceptibly his mouth made contact with hers. While she stood, stunned into stillness, he raised his head and looked down at her, the faintest smile on his face, then he lifted his hand to tuck a silky strand of blonde hair back into place behind her ear. '*Dormi bene*. Sleep well, my sweet.'

He opened the door, snapped on a light and gestured her past him with a glint of mockery in his grey eyes, then shut the door behind her.

She leaned against the wooden panels, listening as his footsteps receded, her clammy fingers outspread for support, her eyes wide and staring like some hunted animal. What on earth was wrong with her? She was shaking inside, her legs weak and unsteady, and yet Alex had barely touched her... But even when he was at his most laid-back, he still exuded that granite-hard toughness—that win-at-all-costs ruthlessness. Could it be that just to be in the same room with him, breathe the same air, was enough to terrify the wits out of her? Yes, it was.

Her bedroom, the one she had had last time, was prettily furnished in the same light-coloured oak and summery pale-green curtains and coverlet, yet all at once it was alien territory, dangerous and forbidding. She looked around her, the back of her hand pressed to her mouth as a little whimper broke from her, but then she resolutely straightened up and went through to the small adjoining bathroom.

But that same sense of isolation would not leave her, even when she was lying in bed, the cicadas zizzing in the warm darkness outside her open window. At last, she switched on her overhead light, reached into her bedside cabinet and took out the photograph which she had hidden there so that the maid who unpacked her luggage would not see it.

'Oh, James,' she whispered miserably to the pleasant, smiling face in the silver frame. 'You made it sound so easy, but it's not, not now that I'm here all alone. How is he going to be when I tell him?'

She stared down at the photograph intently, as though it were a talisman to keep at bay the dark foreboding which lurked in the shadows all round her. Then, raising it to her lips, she kissed the cold, lifeless glass with a desperate urgency before sliding it under her pillow and switching off the light.

'Please, darling,' she said aloud into the darkness, 'don't let it be long. Please rescue me soon.'

CHAPTER FIVE

Lori, her mind still blurred with sleep, rolled over, opened her eyes, and looked straight up into Alex's enigmatic gaze. For a moment longer she hung, trapped between sleeping and waking, then, as he moved slightly, she gave a strangled gasp and leapt sideways across the bed away from him.

But then she realised, with a jolt of horror, that at some time in the clammy night—drunk with sleep—she must have dragged off her nightdress and now she lay sprawled across the bed, stark-naked. As a sizzling blush engulfed her from her forehead to her toes, she made a frantic snatch at the sheet and dragged it up to cover herself.

'Don't be embarrassed, *tesoro mio*.' There was a glint of private amusement in his eyes. 'I'm glad to see you so—liberated. I always sleep in the nude myself, of course.' Lori closed her eyes involuntarily against the implication of his words—the thought of that long, lean tanned body stretched out in indolent grace. 'And besides, you are not, by any means, the first young woman I have seen naked. Though none, I freely admit, quite so lovely—with skin so pale, so deliciously fresh, like a perfect fruit hanging ripe on the bough and as yet untasted.'

That slow quivering was stirring inside her again, but somehow she must deny his ego the satisfaction of sensing it.

'What do you want?' she asked stonily.

'To have the pleasure of—*rousing* you.' The urbanity of his words did not disguise their double meaning, and when she tried to meet his gaze head-on, her own eyes flickered and fell. 'And to tell you to get up, now. I'm taking you into Venice.'

Venice... In spite of herself, Lori felt the excitement start to fizz up inside her. Four years ago, she'd fallen under the spell of this most romantic, most magical of cities, and hadn't stopped talking about it for months. Why, she'd even, just the other week, tentatively suggested to James that they might honeymoon here, but he'd smiled indulgently then wrinkled up his nose, saying something about the drains and the polluted water. And now—she bit her lip as the horrible irony of the situation hit her in the face.

Instinctively, she turned to where the photograph was hidden, then saw with horror that part of the silver frame was showing under the pillow. And Alex was already looking at it, frowning slightly. Lori, her heart almost stopping, went to push it out of sight but he was too quick for her. He drew it out, turned it over, and she saw the frown deepen and every line in that hard-edged face harden.

'What the hell is this?' He held up the photograph between finger and thumb.

'I would have thought it was obvious. It's a photo of my fiancé.'

'Perhaps you would care to re-phrase that sentence?' Alex's voice was quiet, dangerously so.

'No, I wouldn't.' Something seemed to snap in her and she threw discretion, her healthy fear of this man, to the four winds. 'You see, whatever you force me into, I still love James.'

He looked at her, his eyes narrowing. 'I think, *amore mio*,' he said softly, 'that it would be wiser for you—and far wiser for him—if you were to relinquish him gracefully. After all, whatever his undoubted—virtues,' his lip curled ever so slightly, 'the servants could hardly mistake him for your current pop idol.'

As she watched, her lips tightening, he slid the photograph into the pocket of his navy silk robe.

He was standing right over her now, and she realised for the first time that beneath the robe he too was naked; it was loosely sashed, revealing a V of tanned chest—a tiny sprinkling of dark hairs curling damply from the shower—and parted above the knees by the thrust of a pair of well-muscled thighs.

As every self-preserving instinct in Lori screamed at her to do something—run headlong from the room, leap out of the window, anything—he sat down on the bed, trapping her body against the pull of the sheet, and, putting his hands under her arms, drew her upright. Desperately, she twisted away from him, but he placed one hand on her jaw and tilted her face inexorably towards him, forcing her to meet his scrutiny.

'You wouldn't be getting any—ideas, *angelo mio*, would you?'

'Ideas? I d-don't know what you mean,' she stammered.

'Hmmm.' His fingers tightened on her soft chin, so that she could almost feel the bruises springing up. 'Let me just warn you—if warning is needed—that if *anyone* has any thought of appearing over the horizon on a white charger to rescue his lady fair——'

Rescue! Lori's pulses leapt in shock. Was Alex a mind-reader, on top of everything else?

'Do you mean James?' Miraculously, she managed to sound almost matter-of-fact.

'Of course. Or is there a whole string of admirers waiting in the wings?'

'To rescue me from your clutches, you mean?' she snapped. 'No, there isn't. And you needn't worry, Alex——' she deserved an Oscar for this performance, she really did '——James is far too sensible——'

'Yes, how foolish of me.' His thin lip curled into another sneer. 'The eminently sensible Mr James Forsyth. And yet, for a woman like you——' He left the sentence unfinished, and went on, his voice dropping like acid on her raw nerve-ends, 'And *you* will not, I trust, be so ill-advised as to try any more foolishness with me. For you see, next time there would be no half-measures. I would utterly destroy Paget's, and everyone concerned with them.'

He released his hold on her but, as she lay paralysed by his words, he curved the fingers of his right hand into the palm, as though he were remorselessly crushing something—or someone—to death. 'Do I make myself clear?'

'Yes.' From somewhere she salvaged most of her voice. 'I understand you perfectly, Alex.'

'Good. Of course, this is only for a very short space of time. After that——'

He paused and Lori, in spite of herself, queried, 'After that?'

'Why, after that, we shall be married,' he purred. 'And I intend to ensure that you never again think of James Forsyth, or any other man!'

All at once, Lori's nostrils were filled with the leathery smell of soap, the spicy tang of aftershave, and beneath that another perfume—warm, vibrant and overwhelmingly masculine. It was, so she told herself afterwards a hundred times, because of all those scents, mingling in her, permeating every part of her being, that she made no move of any kind to get away, only gazed up at him, her lips parted, as he bent towards her to take her mouth in a fierce, possessive kiss.

Crushed against his chest, she lay helpless in his grip as first his lips and then his tongue devoured the sweetness of her mouth, giving back to her his own wet sweetness. Her senses swimming, she closed her eyes and a little moan was forced from deep within her throat.

He kept his mouth on hers, but dimly she felt one hand slide down the slender column of her throat, over the thin cotton of the sheet to rest on one of her breasts. Very slowly, he began brushing his palm across it, creating a soft, almost unbearable friction which sent stars reeling through her brain. As her own hands came up to clutch convulsively in the still damp dark hair, she felt against the warmth of his palm her nipple tense and engorge.

Only then did he release her mouth. His lips slid down her throat, dropping tiny nipping caresses on to the heated skin, stretched like a bow-string as, barely consciously, she arched her throat against him. As he took the nipple into his mouth she tensed, then, when he caught it between his teeth, a shudder—half of pain, half of delicious thrill—racked her whole body.

But he shouldn't. He mustn't! Lori, though, drowning in that turbulent sea of bewildering sensation, could only cling to him and, as the voices of Elena's two sons arguing outside on the terrace floated up through the open window, it was Alex who broke away at last while she stared up at him, her eyes blank.

His own eyes were very dark. 'Well, well.'

The faintest note of irony underscored his voice and it roused her instantly. An intense blush flared up over her entire body, its heat scalding her.

'How dare you k-kiss me like that?' she exclaimed. 'It—it's disgusting.' The disgust, though, was all for herself.

Alex quirked a black brow. 'You did not seem to find it disgusting a moment ago, but if that is what you wish to believe—my apologies.' He did not look in the least apologetic. 'Certainly, if my mother were to have come in, she would have been scandalised by my behaviour.' He gave her a slanted smile. 'She might even have insisted on our marrying today instead of in three days' time.'

'Three days!' Her anger and shame were lost in the shocked disbelief. 'But you can't, can you?' Stupid question, of course—Alex could do anything.

'It can be arranged. My lawyer will be here shortly and he will require your signature to complete the formalities. So yes, the wedding is in three days. We discussed it last night, after you left us, and the family agreed with me——' well, that figured; no doubt they'd agree that the moon was made of Gorgonzola cheese if Alex told them so '—that it will be better this way. A fitting climax, don't you agree,' he added sardonically, 'to our whirlwind romance?'

'But my father——'

'I have already telephoned your father and he is arriving on the evening flight tomorrow. We shall meet him at the airport and take him to my town house.'

'So, all that's been taken care of, as well.' Her voice was spiked.

'Naturally.' Alex spread his expressive hands. 'A bride should have no worries—apart from ensuring that she looks at her most beautiful for her bridegroom, of course.'

'Well, hadn't you better nail down your silver and anything else of value?'

'And why should I do that?'

'Dad and I will be on the loose in your house,' she said bitterly. 'A couple of thieves like us.'

'Now that I have met your father, I realise that I misjudged him,' Alex said coolly.

'Oh.' She looked at him, a dazzling smile breaking on her face.

'He is, I am sure, an honourable man. Naïve, perhaps, in the world of business, but honest.'

'Well, I told you that all along, didn't I? And that means you don't think that I...?' She faltered into silence, the wild hope almost suffocating her.

'Stole my designs? I did not say that, *cara*.' The regret, she could have sworn, was genuine—almost. 'What I am prepared to believe is that your theft was not part of a pre-arranged plot, but a spur-of-the-moment decision. You saw your chance and snatched at it.'

'So I'm still a thief.' The acid bile of disappointment spurted through her, and she gave a bitter laugh. 'What a basis for a marriage. You think I'm a thief, and I—well, you know the way I feel about you.'

'And how do you feel about me?' That darkly handsome face was very near hers, but somehow she met his ironic gaze unflinchingly.

'I loathe you, hate you, detest you, of course. Will that do?'

He gave her that slow cat's smile. 'Ah, but do you? Are you quite sure that you know how you feel about me?'

'Yes, of course I am. And very soon you'll see just how I——' She broke off, her palms clammy with sudden terror. In her anger and let-down, she'd almost been lured into giving herself—and James—away.

'Just how you——?' he prompted, his eyes narrowing slightly.

'Oh, nothing.'

'Hmmm.' He studied her face for a long moment. 'But in any case, *carissima*, while you tell me one thing, your body——' almost lazily, he brushed a finger across the line where the sheet was wrapped tightly across her chest '—tells me quite another.'

She bit hard on the soft inside of her mouth as she realised that, at his barely perceptible touch, her breasts were tensing once more, the nipples hardening and springing up as though yearning for a further caress— and she realised also that he knew it too.

He glanced at her small bedside clock. 'Luigi Mannini, my lawyer, will be here in half an hour—and then we will leave for Venice.'

Even as he closed the door, a shudder ran through her. She jack-knifed up in bed, staring blank-eyed at the opposite wall, as terror engulfed her. It still wasn't too late. She could refuse to sign the papers, tell the lawyer that she was being blackmailed into this as the last chilling act of Alex's vendetta, and the marriage could be called off, even now. But no—she had to go through with it, for her father's sake, for Paget's. If she gave Alex the least excuse, he would have not the slightest compunction in carrying out his threat and destroying them all.

And James's comforting theory as to Alex's behaviour, once they were married: that rape, or anything like it, would be way beneath him...? It had seemed convincing enough at the time, but now that she was here, in the front line of battle...

She ran a dry tongue around chalky lips. Would Alex even have to resort to forcing himself on her? He was a devil, a master of seduction. If she hadn't guessed it before, she knew it now. And he'd been using only a fraction of his powers—operating on less than one cylinder. How could she so easily have all but given in, betraying herself and James?

Her eyes fell to the sheet and she saw the faint circle of damp where, with only his tongue, his teeth, he had caressed her to the very edge of oblivion. The mark of shame...

Her finger traced around it, then, flinging back the sheet abruptly, she climbed out of bed and went through to the bathroom to shower.

As the water taxi nudged against the quay, Alex leapt lithely out then extended a firm hand to help Lori before peeling a wad of notes from his wallet and handing them to the driver. Typical Alex Baresi. When they'd arrived at the landing stage people had been piling on to a *vaporetto*, just like the ones she'd used four years ago when she'd gone sight-seeing alone. But Alex had imperiously steered her towards this private water taxi. Horrendously expensive—much faster though, and that was the name of the game for this man, wasn't it?

But her annoyance had evaporated as they'd made their way along the Grand Canal, the old excitement rising in her as, on each side, they'd passed the domed churches, the carved stone façades of elegant, fairy-tale Renaissance houses and *palazzi*, with their red and white striped mooring poles, the sleek black gondolas bobbing alongside.

And now, as Alex straightened up, she turned away and, exactly as four years ago, her breath was knocked clean out of her lungs by the sheer physical impact of St Mark's Square.

'It—it's wonderful,' she murmured shakily.

'Yes, it is.' His tone was offhand but she was not deceived. Like all Venetians, lurking just below the casual surface were pride and a fiercely possessive love for their native city. Suppose that fierce possessiveness was turned in another direction? Alex's wife, for instance...

Alex slid a hand under her elbow and steered her across the square. Although it was still early, the temperature was rising rapidly so that the heat came up at them from the grey and white paving, and Lori was glad that she had decided on the fine voile dress, coolly patterned in sea-washed shades of green and blue. Alex, too, was casually dressed, though still sleekly elegant in lightweight grey cords and white shirt.

There were quite a few tourist groups in the square already, gathered like nervous sheep around their shepherds, briskly efficient guides. Flocks of pigeons were wheeling above them and someone had thrown down handfuls of corn. As Lori halted, her way blocked by dozens of feeding birds, one circled then landed on her shoulder, and when she gently put out her hand another settled on her palm, cooing softly. Smiling, she turned to Alex and saw that he was watching her, no answering smile on his face but instead a strange intentness.

For a moment, the tourists, the pigeons—everything faded. Then, her little involuntary jerky movement sent the birds fluttering off. A second later, they were walking under the tiled mosaics of the cathedral as if nothing had happened, yet Lori's pulses were hammering, her breath erratic.

They turned down one of the narrow alleys and Alex led her into a jeweller's shop. The proprietor came forward instantly.

'Signor Baresi, *signorina*——' a smile and a courteous little bow in her direction '—may I congratulate you both?'

Well, well, Lori thought ironically, good news travels fast in Venice.

'I wish to see some engagement rings, please,' Alex said crisply.

I—not we!

As the jeweller took up his keys, in a cold, clear little undertone she said, 'Really, there's no need—for such a *short* engagement.'

But Alex merely slanted her that infuriating smile. 'If you prefer, regard it as an eternity ring.'

Eternity! But she wasn't going to be here for eternity.

'If I'm to have one at all—I'll have a diamond.' She darted Alex a smouldering look from under her lashes. 'I had a nice diamond ring once. I like diamonds.'

He lifted one shoulder by half an inch. 'But of course, my sweet—in their place. And their place is not on your third finger.' Turning to the jeweller, he said, 'I'll see some emeralds.'

While they waited, Lori rested her left hand on the counter, her fingers tapping irritably. During the water taxi ride, Alex had finally removed his ring, replacing it on his own hand, and for an odd little moment her finger looked quite bare. It was amazing what you could get used to; presumably slaves soon became accustomed to their chains.

A tray of emerald rings was set before them. Alex picked over them perfunctorily, then shook his head. 'No, there's nothing here.'

Lori sucked in her breath in a soundless gasp, cringing on behalf of the jeweller's wounded feelings. But he was obviously used to dealing with the great and rich of this world.

'If Signor Baresi will wait a moment, I have one other ring. It's rather special.' Unlocking a wall safe, he took out a small leather box, opened it and with a little flourish laid the ring on the white suede cushion in front of them. Without comment, Alex picked it up and slid it on to her finger.

She stared down at it, her mouth forming a small 'O' of wonderment. The huge emerald was square-cut, in a plain setting of dark gold, and against her pale, slim hand it glowed like green fire, frozen yet at the same time flickering with warmth as it reflected the lights overhead.

Dimly, she heard the man say, 'It is quite flawless. I have rarely seen a stone so perfect.'

'I'll take it.'

No, don't, she thought, a spasm of guilt running through her. Nothing so sordid as money was mentioned, but the number of *lire* notes this fabulous ring would cost would surely stretch from here to the moon and halfway back. And in a few months it would be off her finger and James's ring in its place...

But, even as she opened her mouth to protest, his hand closed over hers, the ring cutting into her soft skin.

'I also want a wedding-ring for my fiancée—and one for myself.'

* * *

As soon as they were out of the shop, she rounded on him. 'Why did you buy it? I told you that I wanted a diamond, but you——'

'Because it is the exact colour of your eyes—when you are angry with me.'

'Oh!' Lori, thoroughly thrown for a moment, struggled to recover. 'But it was the most expensive in the shop.'

'I hope so.'

He was striding ahead through a tiny square, she trotting breathlessly to keep up with his long legs. A fountain was playing in the centre of the *piazza* and just for a moment she was tempted to tear the emerald from her finger and fling it into the opaque pool, in a mirror gesture of his contemptuous disposal of James's ring—that neat, pretty ring with its hoop of diamonds. But then, at the thought of Alex's reaction, her heart quailed, and the ring stayed firmly in place.

He turned down another narrow street and drew up alongside a shop window containing just one dress, a deceptively nothing of a creation in black silk, a pink feather boa floating from it.

'Right,' he said briskly. 'Your new wardrobe starts here.'

Now she really did have a chance to assert herself. 'But I don't want a new wardrobe.' She'd been working on this little speech ever since he'd told her, that night at Mallards, to dump most of her clothes, so it came out very fluently. 'You see, I wear jeans and T-shirts or sweatshirts most of the time. So it would just be a waste——'

'Ah, but as my wife you will not wear jeans and T-shirts most of the time. Sloppy clothes may have been fine for your lifestyle in England, but they will not be appropriate for the wife of Alessandro Baresi. So——'

And before she had time to plant her mutinous feet firmly on the cobbles, she was on the other side of the glass door...

'Bene.' Alex glanced down at his watch. 'Lunchtime, I think.'

They were back by St Mark's Square again, and Lori's gaze went automatically to the crowded café tables spilling out all round the square.

'No, not here.' He was fishing out from his back pocket a rolled up pale-grey silk tie. 'We'll eat at the Danieli Hotel.'

And he was steering her through the throng of sightseers and along the Riva degli Schiavoni.

CHAPTER SIX

THE hotel's roof garden restaurant was cool and shaded. Lori took a sip of mineral water and leaned back in her chair. Almost at their feet, it seemed, was the lagoon, lost in a soft heat-haze, and out of it floated the island of San Giorgio Maggiore, the superb outline of its church shimmering like a beautiful, intangible dream. Perfect, heart-aching beauty. A smile curved her lips and unthinkingly she turned to share the pleasure of the moment with Alex.

Fortunately, though, he was studying the elaborate menu card, and, pulling herself up, Lori let her eyes wander instead to their fellow diners. How was it that they all, somehow, were managing to exude that subtly understated opulence of the genuinely rich? The women's clothes helped, of course—casually chic, 'designer' written all over them...

Her simple voile dress just about passed muster, although some of the outfits at this very moment on their way to Alex's town-house would certainly have been better... Those elegant little silk suits and shirts, that hot-pink crepon empire-line dress, the jade-green linen suit. Any one of those would have been perfect. Maybe not the Valentino dress, though, she thought, with a private smile. Full-length, in sealing-wax red, one shoulder bare, slashed up to the thigh, so that every step she took was almost indecent...

In spite of herself, a little shiver of excitement ran through her. But then, at the memory of those other purchases—those dainty little scraps of coffee, ivory and cream lace and silk that seemed to pass for bra and pants—she swallowed against a sudden obstruction in her throat. And those nightdresses and négligés... As she'd turned, surveying herself in the gilt-mirrored changing-room, she'd realised for the first time in her life—and with a start of real fear—just how right was the saying that a woman's body was far more desirable slightly veiled, its curves and hollows only hinted at—

'Are you ready to order?' Alex was regarding her over the top of his menu card.

'Oh, n-not quite.' And she buried her nose in her own menu...

'I like your earrings.'

Lori looked up from her delicious creamy lobster mousse. 'Oh, I made them myself.'

Alex held out an imperious hand. 'Let me see.'

Putting down her fork, she unscrewed one of the dainty pink glass spirals and dropped it into his hand.

'It isn't perfect,' she said defensively. 'I got an air bubble into it.'

He held it up to the light. Against his strong hands, the little bauble looked incongruous. 'Do you produce these commercially?'

'Not really. I've made some for friends, but it's more of a hobby. I just enjoy making them.' She pulled a face. 'It's the nearest I get to actual glass-making since I left college. I concentrate on design now.'

She could have bitten her tongue off, but he only nodded wryly. 'I know the feeling. I sell the stuff—and that means I spend most of my life in offices or planes, but once in a while my fingers physically itch to get to grips with a blob of molten glass.' He dropped the earring into her palm. 'But these could go really well. I'll set you up with a kiln.'

'Oh, no, really.' For a moment, Lori felt quite distressed. For the last few moments she and Alex had seemed almost on the same wavelength, linked by their knowledge and love of glass. Now, though, 'I'd rather you didn't,' she said awkwardly. There were already more than enough ties being woven around her to bind her to Venice and the Baresis without being bound further by delicate threads of glass.

As she screwed the earring back into place the reflected sunlight from the silver champagne bucket caught the emerald on her finger, turning it to brilliant green fire. And, just as the ring was dazzling her, so Alex was setting out quite deliberately to dazzle her.

'It won't work, you know,' she said abruptly.

'What?' One dark eyebrow was raised in delicate enquiry.

'I know perfectly well what you're doing. This ring, those horrendously expensive clothes, this gorgeous lunch in a fifteenth-century Doge's palace.' Her sweeping gesture took in the surrounding tables. 'Bringing me here to rub shoulders with all these Beautiful People.' Her lips twisted. 'Everything so carefully calculated.'

'To achieve what?' His grey eyes were trained disconcertingly on her now, but she would not be put off.

'To show me, of course, that all I have to do is be the docile little wife of Alex Baresi, and all this will be mine.'

'And so it shall be. You have mapped out your future impeccably, *carina*.' A light, totally infuriating smile was playing round his lips.

'But supposing I don't want that kind of future?' she retorted bitterly. 'You must think I'm still a child, tempting me with lollipops.'

'A child? Oh, no, *amore mio.*' His voice dropped to an intimate murmur. 'I no longer think of you as a child—not after this morning, I promise you.'

Instantly, the colour zinged to her cheeks, but she bit back any further response—after all, with Alex's catlike intuition she'd said more than enough already. If she totally lost control, she could easily blow her and James's plan sky high. And Paget's with it.

So instead she contented herself with stabbing viciously at the meltingly tender salmon trout which had just been slid unobtrusively in front of her.

Alex halted in a handkerchief-sized square and Lori gazed around the tiny *piazza.* It was cobbled, an ancient stone well in the centre, and across one corner a narrow canal, whose opaque green water gave back zigzag reflections of the tall buildings on the other three sides.

Butting on to the canal was a beautiful house—four storeys, painted in softly glowing ochre. The upper windows were closely shuttered, the lower ones open on to a stone-balustraded balcony lined with tubs of scarlet geraniums and small clipped bay trees.

Alex reached into his pocket and took out a key which he inserted into the huge wooden front door. It swung open to reveal a black and white marble hall, a curving staircase disappearing into the shadows above. He gestured her in past him.

'Welcome to your new home, *cara.*'

But for once Lori was almost oblivious to the slightly sardonic tone. That third glass of champagne he'd pressed on her at lunch, and then that labyrinth of alleyways and bridges they'd plunged into after leaving the hotel—they'd combined to blow her mind completely. She stared at him, jaw sagging.

'This is your house?' And, when he shrugged acknowledgement, 'But—it's a *palazzo*.'

'A small one, yes.'

As she stepped into the deliciously cool hall an elderly woman, dressed in black, appeared.

'This is Olga Cerezo, my housekeeper.'

Gesturing towards Lori, he said something to the woman, and her face was wreathed in an instant smile. Somehow Lori summoned an answering smile and Signora Cerezo broke into a flood of Italian. Finally, Alex cut in.

'She says, would you like a cold drink?'

'Oh.' Lori turned to the woman. 'Er—*no, grazie, signora*.'

'Later, perhaps.' He paused, then added casually, 'She also says that my bride is very beautiful.'

Lori, covered in confusion, could only give the housekeeper another forced smile. Alex spoke a few swift words to her and she gave a little bobbing curtsy, then retreated.

'Now, let me show you round your new home.'

'For heaven's sake——' Lori's nerves were at snapping-point '—do you have to keep saying that—my new home, I mean?'

'But that, my sweet, is precisely what it is.'

Alex opened one of the doors leading off the hall and she found herself in a large, beautifully proportioned room, its high ceiling and cornices patterned with intricately moulded plaster-work. Over the huge fireplace was a carved stone tablet, on which the same two lions—of Venice and the Baresis—which snarled out of Alex's signet ring faced each other again, front paws joined.

High windows gave out on to the balcony and beyond that was the narrow canal and the stone façade of the house opposite. The room was superbly—even opulently—furnished, but all Lori's attention went immediately to the mahogany cabinet and she took an instinctive step towards it.

Behind her, Alex laughed softly. 'Yes, I rather thought you would find that more interesting than the English Hepplewhite chairs and seventeenth-century Florentine hangings.'

'Oh, of course,' she said tightly. 'My thief's eye sussing out the priceless Venetian glass, I suppose.'

Alex gave a faint sigh, then, putting his hands on her shoulders, turned her to him. 'You know, *cara*, you really must stop seeing veiled insults behind every word I speak.'

'Must I?' she said defiantly, but her eyes could get no further up than the second button of his shirt. The cotton was so fine that, beneath it, she could see the almost imperceptible beat of his heart.

'Yes, you must. And certainly, in this case, all I meant was that, as two professionals, we share a love of exquisite glass.' He opened the double-fronted cabinet. 'Please feel free.'

Hardly breathing, Lori took out one of the pieces, a wide, shallow bowl of iridescent glass, its centre glowing with greenish-gold fire.

'You have a good eye.' Alex was watching her as she ran one fingertip reverently over the smooth base.

'It's very lovely.'

'It's the oldest piece I have. It was made by the Baresi who founded our firm in 1643—another Alessandro. He made it for his wife-to-be, Lucia Vialli.'

Lori grimaced. 'In that case, I think I'd better put it back.'

As she carefully replaced it, he went on, 'Most of the items here were made for Baresi brides. After Alessandro, it became a kind of tradition in our family. My mother still cherishes the piece which my father made for her just before their wedding. In our case, unfortunately, there was no time.'

Again, she could not quite meet his eye. 'Was it another bowl?'

'No.' His voice was neutral. 'He made her a loving cup. You must ask her to show it to you.'

But Lori knew instantly that she wouldn't. The sharp contrast of that wedding and theirs—surely, nothing could throw it into more poignant relief than a beautiful glass loving cup, created by love for a pair of lifelong lovers. Biting her lip against a sudden, almost over-whelming sadness, she reclosed the cabinet.

Back in the hall, Alex paused. 'Most of the main rooms are on the first and second floors, but before that——'

Opening another door, he led her down a flight of modern pine steps, slid back a glass partition, flicked a light switch and instantly a small swimming-pool was revealed, the water glowing brilliant aquamarine from the underwater lighting. At the far end was a white trellis with potted plants—palms, yucca and a trailing plumbago, its blue-starred branches reaching to the ceiling. Beyond the trellis was a pine sauna cabin and a changing-room, a black towelling robe tossed down on the bench.

Lori gave a startled laugh.

'You approve, I trust?' Alex asked drily.

'Yes, it's gorgeous. It's just—well, it's so incongruous in a sixteenth-century *palazzo*.'

'I had it installed a couple of years ago—the best way I know to shake off the tensions of a session with difficult clients. And now, the rest of the house.'

The curving staircase to the first floor was hung with pale peach watered silk, a perfect foil to the oil-paintings in their gilded frames. But, as they climbed, the only sensation Lori felt was a spiralling panic. Whether Alex was doing it deliberately or not, the end result was the same. The casual display of wealth—this fabulous house, oozing opulence from every pore, exactly as its owner did—how could she stand up against it? She'd never cared overmuch for money, happily wearing jeans, driving a beat-up old Mini, preferring fast-food takeaways to glossy restaurants—in fact, she'd been aware that this carefree attitude often irritated James—but now suddenly she began to feel afraid.

Despite her defiant words over lunch, if she wasn't very careful, all this—a state dining-room, then, up another flight of stairs, a charming, sunny sitting-room which Alex said would be hers, her own private dressing-room and bathroom, the sunken bath in pale marble—all this would completely turn her head . . .

Alex threw open yet another door. A bedroom. A huge bed, with a carved head. On the cream silk coverlet were piled silver-wrapped packages—her new wardrobe, safely delivered.

'You like it?'

'Er—yes.' But her eyes were taking in the dark wood of the furnishings, the austere wallpaper.

'You can make changes if you wish, of course.'

'Oh, thank you, but——' she said awkwardly.

'Though I must say that I wouldn't care particularly to sleep in pink chintz.'

'Oh, I'm sorry.' She coloured slightly with embarrassment. 'With my clothes here, I thought this was my bedroom.'

'But it is,' he replied smoothly. 'Or rather—in three nights' time, at least—ours.'

'Oh, but——' The colour had surged, peony-pink, into her cheeks now.

'Yes, I know that you will be disappointed to be deprived of a honeymoon.' Was there the faintest undertone of irony? 'But with everything being arranged at such short notice——' there was no doubt about the irony now '—I'm afraid I have two very important meetings, which I cannot postpone. We'll take a holiday later—anywhere you wish—but in the meantime I promise I shall do my best to—er—make up for any disappointment you might feel.'

Lori's entire body seemed to jerk convulsively, her eyes flicking to the bed, then away just as quickly. After days of being almost wrapped in a dream—or rather, nightmare—she'd finally woken up. This room, this bed, was to be their battleground. And, without bringing ruin on her father and herself, there was no way she could avoid it.

To try and cover the agitation which churned inside her, she walked across to the window. It was half shuttered, but through the gap she had an oblique view down the narrow canal and out to the lagoon, still wrapped in the glare of afternoon heat.

'Th-that island there. Is it——?'

'Yes, it's Murano.' Alex had soundlessly crossed the room—like a stalking panther, she thought involuntarily—and now his voice came from just behind her. Every muscle in her tensed, but she did not turn round. 'I'll take you out there to our works soon.'

The last time she'd been there was that terrible final afternoon, in Alex's design studio, when he thought she'd stolen——

'You can see the factory from here, on a clear day.'

'How useful for you.' Her voice was brittle. 'To keep a close eye on your work-force, I mean.'

'I could do, yes,' he agreed evenly, 'but that is not necessary.'

His breath was curling about her neck, stirring the fine hairs, and abruptly she moved away from the window towards the far wall where, for the first time, she saw a painting hanging. She stared at it in amazement. The Renoir in the dining-room, the Matisse in the salon—Alex had carelessly assured her that yes, of course they were originals, but this one—surely not?

'I'm afraid I couldn't persuade the Uffizi to part with the real thing.' The wry smile was apparent in his voice. 'But this is an excellent copy, don't you agree?'

She went slowly up to it, taking in the lovely woodland scene, the flimsily clad nymphs, Cupid hovering above that wonderfully serene Venus. And then Flora, Spring herself, the long blonde hair, the green eyes, the full sensual mouth, that ravishing flower-sprigged dress matching the diadem of flowers in her hair... 'You know, Lorina, with those wide, sea-green eyes and those flowers in your hair, you look just like Botticelli's *Primavera* ...'

She turned slowly towards him, her lips parted, and saw Alex watching her, a strange expression on his face.

'Lori,' he began huskily, but then, as the silence hung heavy between them, the sound of voices reached them from the entrance hall two floors below, and with an odd little grimace he turned away.

'Signorina Giannini.' He glanced at his watch. 'Right on time.'

As Lori looked at him in puzzlement, he jerked his thumb towards one of the boxes on the bed. It was different from the others—old and battered-looking. 'Take a look.'

It was a command, and she moved slowly to the bed, lifted the lid, and instantly the scent of lavender and woodruff drifted up to her from among the layers of white tissue. With a growing sense of unease, she parted the tissue, then gazed questioningly up at him.

'Well, go on. Lift it out.' There was a faint crackle in his voice, not exactly of impatience, more of tension.

The dress was as fragile and insubstantial as a cobweb, the lace, not pure white but the delicate creamy white of buttermilk, cascading down as she took it out.

'It is Venetian lace,' he said softly, 'from the island of Burano. Every stitch hand-done, of course.'

'But what is it?' she whispered.

'The Baresi wedding dress. It was made over a century ago, and since then every Baresi bride has worn it.'

That panic was rising again. The Baresi wedding dress—one more link in the chain binding her to this man.

'No!' she said loudly. 'I won't wear it!'

His black brows contracted. 'Why not?'

'Well,' in the face of his sudden anger, she prevaricated, 'for one thing, I'm sure it won't fit me. As your mother keeps telling me, I'm terribly thin.'

'And that is precisely why Signorina Giannini is here. She's my mother's dressmaker.'

Right on cue, there was a soft knock at the door, and Alex, his eyes daring her to protest further, called, 'Avanti.'

If Lori had expected to see a little old lady in black, clutching a tape measure, she was wrong. Signorina

Giannini was a young woman, elegantly slim in a floral print silk suit and high heels, carrying an executive-style case.

'*Buongiorno*, Signor Baresi. Good afternoon, Miss Paget.'

Lori, still totally thrown, could only mumble a response.

Alex turned to her. 'I will leave you, *cara*.' He slanted them both a smile which, Lori noticed sourly, at least had the desired effect on the dressmaker. While her own face stayed frozen, the young woman almost simpered. 'It is bad luck, so I'm told, for the groom to see his bride in her wedding dress before she floats down the aisle towards him, a vision of loveliness.'

Only Lori was aware of the ironic undertone. She could not trust her voice, and instead shot him a private look of loathing from under her lashes. But Alex did not apparently see it for, taking her hand, he raised it to his lips, bending his head to kiss it. She tried to draw away, but his grip tightened, and turning her hand over he brushed his lips sensuously across the palm, finally nipping the rounded flesh at the base of her thumb, until Lori, her eyes closing, felt her pulses begin to quicken, her treacherous body once more stir into life.

When he released her, she jerked her hand away, her face on fire, to see Signorina Giannini regarding them both indulgently.

'*A più tardi, carissima,*' he murmured. '*Signorina——*' he made her a formal little bow '—I shall see you before you leave, of course.'

As the door closed, Lori glanced at the other woman and was astonished to see on her pretty face an expression of almost mindless adoration. The adoration, she thought savagely, of the Helpless Little Woman for

the Sleek Handsome Male Animal. Signorina Giannini,
he eats people, that one, she was tempted to say. Eats
them, mangles them body and soul, then spits out the
pips.

Their glances met, and Lori saw now in the brown
eyes a look, not exactly of envy, more of wry acknowledgement that she, Lori, had scooped the jackpot. Then
the dressmaker, all brisk efficiency, set down her case
on the bed.

'Now, Miss Paget, if you would be so kind as to take
off your dress.'

Lifting the wedding dress for Lori to step into, she
drew it up around her, then hooked up the dozens of
tiny silk buttons down her back. The body of the dress
was silk, the bodice covered with lace flowers. The skirt,
too, was covered with layers of ruched lace, narrow
ruffles at the waist shading to larger ones at the train.
At the heart of every flower a seed pearl had been sewn,
like a translucent tear drop.

The woman circled her slowly, lips pursed. 'I think
Signor Baresi will be well satisfied with his bride.' She
flashed Lori a quick smile. 'When I have taken in these
side-seams, of course.' She was deftly pinning in the material. 'I shall take the dress with me now and bring it
to the villa tomorrow evening. Signora Baresi wishes to
check it herself and, of course, her hairdresser is coming
to decide on the best style to go with the veil.' She gestured towards a mound of lace still lying in the bottom
of the box. 'He is due at six, I think.'

She looked enquiringly at Lori who thought, with a
stab of resentment, Don't ask me, please. I'll be the last
to know. But she managed, 'Y-yes, I think so.'

Taking her by the shoulders, the woman guided her across to a full-length mirror. 'It is truly beautiful, isn't it?'

Lori, though, was barely conscious of her voice. She was seeing the way the scoop neckline and slightly puffed sleeves set off her face and shoulders, the spreading skirts emphasised her fine-boned slenderness, and the creamy-white fabric complemented her delicate skin and wide green eyes.

But there was something more than that. The dress was magic; it had to be. For when, half fearfully, she met the eyes of her other self, it had cast a glow on to her face, giving her surely the joyful radiance that all happy brides had. But in her case that was utterly impossible.

'Oh, Miss Paget.' Behind her, Signorina Giannini gave a sentimental sigh which should have set Lori's teeth on edge. But, for some reason, it twisted instead at her heart-strings and brought a dangerous moistness to her eyes. 'You look——'

CHAPTER SEVEN

'—ABSOLUTELY wonderful, my dear.' Abruptly, Lori's father cleared his throat, then gave a soft sigh. 'If only your mother could have been here to see her beautiful daughter on her wedding day.'

'Oh, Dad, please don't.' Lori, tension writhing inside her like angry serpents, put her hand quickly on his arm. Somehow she managed a brittle smile. 'You'll have us both in tears in a minute. Anyway, you look pretty fetching yourself.'

'Oh, and—er—James——' every muscle in her body tensed '—rang me before I left. He said to give you his best wishes, and that he's sure everything will turn out well for you. I must say, he seems to have taken it all very well.'

'Yes,' Lori agreed non-committally. Loyal James, beavering away at the rescue plan. That cryptic little message had been reassurance, just in case she needed it—and she certainly did.

'Lori.' Her father took both her hands in his and gazed earnestly at her. 'You do want to marry Alex, don't you?'

Just for a second, the temptation was almost too much. To rush upstairs, tear off this beautiful—hateful—wedding dress and flee to the airport, back to England—and James... Alex was marrying her for revenge, and surely this would be the perfect counter-coup—his humiliation at being left waiting literally at the altar steps, the cream of Venetian society looking on.

But no. She thrust the thought from her and met her father's anxious gaze full on. 'Of course I want to, Dad. I wouldn't be doing it otherwise.'

Her eyes slid past him, and she saw them both reflected in the huge gilt mirror on the opposite wall of the *palazzo*. He, dignified, immaculate in his pale grey morning suit; she, icily composed but very pale, in spite of the colour which Signora Baresi had insisted on dabbing on her cheeks just before she left for the church, in a cloud of Fendi perfume and Marina Rinaldi silk. The marble floor was striking chill through her white glacé pumps and she shivered, but then, mercifully, the front door opened.

'Time to go, my dear,' she heard her father murmur.

Someone carefully lifted her veil over her face, another pair of hands held out her spray of white freesias and orchids, and then she was outside in the brilliant sunlight. Like an actress who had learned her part perfectly, she walked across the tiny square and stepped into the motor launch, to be taken up the narrow canal where people leaned out of their windows, smiling and applauding, and into the Piazza Santa Maria dei Miracoli, the whole of Venice like a painted theatre backdrop to the drama unfolding in its midst.

Above her head, the church's glorious marble façade glowed, then into the cool interior where Alex's three sisters, very solemn-eyed for once in their long dark blue silk dresses, were waiting. Signorina Giannini was there too, adjusting the folds of her dress and veil, straightening the long train behind her, while she stood motionless.

As the organ swelled to a crescendo and the congregation rose to their feet, she began to move slowly down the aisle. And then she saw Alex, turned to watch her, standing at the foot of the wide cream marble steps which led up to the altar.

Just for a moment, she faltered and stood stock-still. This church, with its coral and grey marble walls, its richly carved pillars, its ceiling adorned in gleaming colours—it couldn't be further removed from the simple country church of her childhood dreams. And yet now, for the very first time, instead of a blur she could see the face of the man waiting for her—the face of Alex. And he looked right, so absolutely right, making her dream complete.

But then, as she felt her father's glance, she recovered herself. Of course he looked right, but only because he was here in this exotic Italian church, in his cream tussore silk suit, a shaft of light striking his black hair, illuminating the handsome face and glinting off those opal-grey eyes—which were watching her as she began to move forward once more.

Priests, gorgeous in white and gold, were stepping forward. Marcello was there beside Alex, but she only dimly saw them, quite unable to tear her eyes from his. When she reached him, he held out a hand and, releasing her father's arm, she gave him her icy fingertips, then together they went up the steps, her lace train making little shush-shush sounds behind her. And then the service began, lost for ever in a blur of incense, candles and singing.

She only roused fully once, when Alex slid the ring on to her finger. Her hands were still icy cold but his were warm, and she could feel the life flooding through them. She went rigid. What on earth was she doing, allowing this man who despised her as a worthless thief, who was marrying her solely for revenge, the final act of his latest business coup, to put a wedding-ring on her finger? She stared down at the gold band—the last link in the chain to bind her to him. But it wasn't, she told herself. Not quite the last—and she was going to deny him that final act of subjection.

Mechanically, she took the ring which the priest was holding out to her and went to put it on Alex's finger. It jammed at the knuckle and she had to take hold of his hand. She glanced up to meet his eyes, as cool and shuttered as ever. And yet—just for a split second—she glimpsed another expression, which turned her mouth ash-dry and set her pulses beating crazily with fear.

Hastily, she shielded her eyes with her lashes, but spent the rest of the service trying vainly to erase the memory of that look. It was the way he had looked at her in the villa garden four years ago, and again at Mallards during that terrible take-over meeting. It told her that, amid all the elaborate ritual and formality going on around them, he wanted her, desired her.

In the vestry, she watched as he put his rapid, bold signature to the church and civil registers, and then it was her turn. This was the last time she would write Lorina Jane Paget; from now on it would be Lorina Baresi. But soon it would be Mrs James Forsyth, she told herself fiercely, and the pen sputtered into a tiny shower of inky blots.

Back down the marble steps, this time on Alex's arm, then down the aisle, that smile superglued into place, and out into the sunshine once more, to a cascade of scented rose petals and the clicking cameras of the world's Press.

Just once, the smile slipped abruptly. Among the mass of guests, photographers, tourists who were crowded into the small *piazza*, spilling on to the little bridge which arched over the canal, suddenly one face leapt out at her in crystal clarity. James's face. She stared, rigid in every muscle, then, as she sensed Alex turn to look at her, she dragged her eyes away. When, seconds later, her gaze went back magnet-like to that spot, he had vanished.

A mirage—it must have been, conjured up by her own overwrought imagination. Standing there, by her husband's side, she'd been hallucinating over the face of the man she loved...

At last, she realised that Alex was leading her through the throng towards the edge of the square where a gondola, decked with flowers and white ribbons, was moored. Stepping lightly aboard, he turned and handed her down into it. She sank down on the seat, the beautiful dress billowing around her, and he sat beside her, so close that his arm brushed hers, his leg moved against hers, and through the thin silk she felt his hip and the muscles of his thigh.

As the gondola glided smoothly away he leaned back, one arm casually draped along the back of the seat, and their glances met. He smiled at her, and something about that smile tightened her already overstretched nerves one notch too far so that all her inner tensions suddenly snapped.

'I hope you're satisfied now,' she hissed, conscious of the smiling gondolier with his white-ribboned hat standing just behind them.

'Satisfied? Not entirely, no.' He slanted her another of those catlike smiles. 'But very soon now, I promise you, my sweet.'

At the thought of that final confrontation, her stomach muscles contracted into a tight fist. But she couldn't let him see her fear.

'I suppose you think you've won,' she gritted between her teeth.

'But I have,' he responded softly.

'Have you? Are you quite sure of that?'

'Of course. And really, *cara mia*, there was never any doubt. So——' his voice hardened slightly '—it would be wise of you to accept, once and for all, that you have lost.'

'You think so?' Her voice rose. 'It really doesn't matter to you that I hate you for what you've made me do?'

'Not at all, no. You say I have forced you into marriage as the final act of my vendetta. Very well, then——' and before she could draw back, her took her hand and raised it to his lips '—all that is left for you to do is to—surrender gracefully, my little vendetta bride.'

As the music died away, Marcello whisked her round in a final flourish. Lori smiled up at him, then tensed suddenly as Alex appeared beside them. Since they had formally opened the dancing two hours earlier, he—the perfect host—had assiduously divided his attention among the other guests, and she had actually begun to relax slightly in the security of the crowded salon. Now, though, she immediately felt tension flare inside her once more.

'You permit?' And without waiting for an answer from his brother-in-law Alex slid his arm possessively round her waist and drew her away. When she tried to edge apart from him a little, his fingers tightened on her.

They had sat side by side through that endless wedding breakfast in the *palazzo's* state dining-room, through the speeches, the toasts, Alex perfectly relaxed, her own outward composure as brittle as one of her own glass earrings. When the meal finally ended, in coffee, sweet liqueurs and a haze of cigar smoke, she'd gone upstairs and taken off the Baresi dress. Alex's wedding-ring still encircled her finger, though—if only she could have taken that off as easily.

She'd showered, then dressed for the dance, slipping on one of her new dresses—in fine apricot crêpe, with a low-cut bodice and skirt which softly hugged her slim hips then flared out to just below the knees. As she pulled a comb through her hair, a couple of pink rose petals drifted to the floor. She stood looking down at them for a long time, until Signora Baresi sailed in to see if she needed any help...

Now, as the orchestra struck up a waltz, she tensed herself for Alex to take her in his arms. Instead, he led her out of the salon into the entrance hall and closed the double doors. As he leaned against them, looking down at her, she said jerkily, 'W-we can't possibly leave the reception yet.'

As long as the dancing continued—and no one was showing the slightest inclination to leave for hours yet— the moment of confrontation could be kept at bay. But when she put her hand on the doorknob he placed his own on top of it.

'They're perfectly happy without us. And it's time for us to leave on our honeymoon.'

'Honeymoon?' She stared up at him, aghast. 'But you said we weren't having one.'

'Not a long one, no. But surely——' his voice curled around her '—every bride needs a honeymoon, however brief, to dream about in years to come.'

'Dream about!' She gave a bitter little laugh. 'After the charade of this marriage, believe me, I'm far more likely to have nightmares.'

'We shall see, amore mio, we shall see.' Lifting his hand, he brushed his thumb softly across her lower lip.

'We are spending three nights at the Hotel Cipriani, and our launch is ready to leave.'

From the other side of the door came a burst of music, followed by laughter and a buzz of conversation. In there was safety, while out here, alone with Alex, was danger. But, even as she stared wildly at him, he took her hand and, as she couldn't any longer resist him, led her out to the waiting launch.

Across the strip of inky black water, the lights of Venice twinkled. Lori fixed her eyes on one pale orange oblong, until suddenly it went out. People going to bed. All at once, she shivered and drew more tightly around her slim shoulders the cream silk négligé which she'd found in her case, packed presumably by Signora Cerezo. She turned abruptly away from the window, back to the bedroom.

It was beautifully furnished with antiques, glowing in the soft warmth of the wall lights. They would have graced an international saleroom, but Lori saw only the bed with its superbly carved wooden headboard and its covers already neatly turned down by the chambermaid while she'd been taking her bath.

As she stood staring at it, her fingers twining restlessly among the cream ribbons at her throat, she heard the shower running. Alex. The image of the water cascading down over that tanned, strong body slid terrifyingly into her mind and she stared at the door panels, her green eyes dilated hugely.

Then, as the water was turned off, she gave an almost inaudible sob of fear. Barely aware of what she was doing, she snatched up a pillow from the bed and, running through to the sitting-room, which formed part of their suite, threw herself down on the velvet-covered sofa, clutching it to her.

Her ears strained in the darkness, she heard the bathroom door open and close, there was silence for a few agonising seconds, and then the sitting-room door opened and Alex, in his black silk robe, stood silhouetted against the light. She felt his eyes search through the dimness and finally fix on her, then he leaned in the doorway, arms folded.

'It's bedtime, *cara*,' he said softly.

The moment had come. Thrusting down her fear, she jutted her chin. 'I'm not coming to bed. I'm s-sleeping here.' But she could not wholly keep the tremor from her voice.

She caught a sound, which might have been a laugh, then he was straightening up, coming towards her. He dropped on to the sofa beside her, so close that she was trapped between him and the sofa arm, nowhere to go.

Taking one hand, he held it between his. 'You're cold.'

'No, I'm not. Not at all.'

Her teeth were chattering but it wasn't from cold, and when he brushed his fingers across her wrist she knew that he could feel, beneath the chill skin, her pulse, leaping and bounding like a terrified animal.

His hands on her shoulders, he drew her round to face him. She turned her head away, but, putting one hand to her cheek, he forced her back to meet his eyes.

'Lori.'

'What?' She wanted to sound defiant, but somehow the unaccustomed tenderness in his voice and the gentle smile he gave her were doing dangerous things to her breathing.

He lifted a stray tendril of blonde hair and twined it around his fingers. 'What beautiful hair you have—so soft, so silky. Yet it can bind itself round a man's heart like cords of steel.'

'I'm thinking of having it cut. It's too hot out here for long hair.'

His fingers tightened on the strand until she winced. 'You will not have it cut. Do you hear me?' as she did not reply.

'I'll do as I like.' If her nerves hadn't been stretched to breaking point and beyond, she would never have dared provoke him like this. 'It's my hair.'

She felt the anger flare in him like an electric spark, but then miraculously he relaxed again. 'Oh, Lori.' He gave a rueful little laugh. 'Why is it that I always have to fight down the urge to turn you over my knee and wallop you?'

'I don't know. Probably because you're a sadist,' she muttered.

But he only smiled at her, a smile which rasped against her raw nerve-endings, then taking her hand he gently kissed the palm.

'Trust me, *cara*,' he murmured against the moist skin. 'I know that you are frightened, but I promise that I shall be gentle, and do nothing until you wish it.'

He raised his head, and in the grey eyes she saw that tenderness again, mingled with desire. What a wonderful lover he would be... Just for a moment, she felt a bitter pang of something very like regret, then she slapped down the treacherous thought. Of course he would be, smooth, polished—experienced. And no shadow of doubt had entered his head that she wouldn't very soon be added to his list of easy conquests. Well, she was going to put him straight on that—right now.

But even so, she had to moisten her dry lips before she could speak. 'Alex——'

She got no further. Uncoiling himself, he got to his feet and before she could move had scooped her up into his arms. He held her against him for a moment, looking down at her, then strode through into the bedroom, shouldering open the door, and laid her down on the bed. Immediately, she went to roll away but he caught hold of her by the wrists.

'Let me go,' she panted. 'I've told you—I'm staying in the other room.'

'You will not sleep there tonight.'

'Can't you understand? I'm not going to sleep with you—ever.'

He gazed down at her, eyes narrowed, the pupils so intensely black that she could see tiny images of herself reflecting back at her.

'So the reluctance in there,' he said at last, jerking his head, 'was not, as I imagined, the terror of a timid, inexperienced virgin.' The acid contempt in his voice could have flayed leather.

'How very quick you are,' she flung at him. 'Got it in one.'

In a gesture of barely controlled anger, he released her wrists and they stared into each other's faces. She was very pale, while a thread of dark colour ran along his sharp-edged cheekbones.

'Have you forgotten so soon——' his words fell into the room like chips from an Arctic iceflow '—the vows you made in church just a few hours ago? But perhaps you didn't understand—maybe I should have laid on an interpreter for you.' His lip curled in a sneer.

'Oh, I understood all right. Love, honour and obey— that was it, wasn't it? Or something along those lines?'

The look from those hard grey eyes would have splintered granite, but he was obviously reining in his anger, for all he said was, 'Exactly—to love, honour and obey your husband.'

'Or, to put it another way, to be a good, docile little wife, you m-mean?' Just for a moment, the dreadful enormity of what she was doing made her voice tremble. 'Don't think I didn't hate myself for saying those words, Alex. But you forced me into this. I begged you not to— but no. And an oath made under duress is not in the least binding, as you very well know.'

Alex muttered something that sounded very like a barely suppressed obscenity, then, 'May I remind you, *tesoro*, that you have married me in exchange for——?'

'—the life of Paget Crystal. And——'

'Exactly. I allowed your company to live—and now you will pay your debt to me.'

'But I've done what you demanded. I've married you, haven't I? Or was there something else in the small print of our *business* agreement that I've missed?'

'Don't try to be funny with me.'

But she drove herself on. 'You forced me to marry you, Alex. You can make me obey you, I don't doubt——' instinctively, she glanced down at her wrist, where those marks he had put on her still showed, the faintest blue against the delicate creaminess of her skin '—but you can't make me love you. Love just can't be forced like that. You know that, surely—after all, you don't love me.' She faltered just for a moment, but then went on, 'And in my book, love and sex go together.'

'Oh, and what book is that?' The icy timbre in his voice brought goose pimples of terror out on her nape. 'The *Frigid English Virgin's Bedside Companion*, I suppose.'

The savage gibe almost broke her spirit to resist. 'I w-won't make love to you. You may have bought me, but——'

'Yes, I have. And in my book,' savagely he echoed her words, 'as you're one of my possessions, that gives me exclusive rights to your body.'

'No. I'll be a decorative little wife—that's what a man like you wants, isn't it? You've already loaded me with clothes, with jewellery——' involuntarily, her eyes fell to the emerald ring, blazing green fire '—and I'll do my best to be an ornament for you to show off to all your friends and clients, but I swear I'll be nothing else.'

He looked at her for a moment, then, 'You little bitch,' he said, very quietly. 'I should think carefully—very carefully indeed, before you try to play games with me.'

'Oh, it's no game, Alex, I assure you.' She even managed a careless laugh.

'I may, for example, have to reconsider the position of Paget Crystal.'

'W-what do you mean? You can't——'

'Oh, but I can. Paget's is my company now and, if I choose, I can wipe it from the face of the earth.'

'You cold-blooded swine.'

He lifted a shoulder. 'So you are always telling me.'

She stared at him, chewing frantically at her underlip. The anger was pumping adrenalin round her body, driving her on to defy him, shout in his face, Do what you damn well like, I still won't sleep with you. But somehow she had to control herself. If she unleashed the sleeping tiger of Alex's anger any further, who knew what might happen? Something terrible, for sure.

She drew a deep breath. 'Look, Alex, I meant what I said. I *have* married you, and I promise I'll do my best to be a good wife—in the eyes of the world, at least. And no one need ever know, except us.'

'But you see, you stupid little fool, in this neat little business package you're so generously offering me, you have forgotten one thing.'

'W-what's that?'

'I want children.' He spoke quietly, almost matter-of-factly, but there was no doubting the stark truth behind his words, and there flashed in her mind the image of him holding his baby nephew in his arms, the expression on his face.

'Oh.' It was a frightened breath. And yet... 'He's the kind of dynastic swine' —James's words came to her again, showing her her way of escape.

'Well, you'll just have to get them somewhere else,' she said, amazed at her own apparent coolness. 'And if it's an heir to the precious Baresi empire that you're looking for, you'll have to marry someone else. After all, you'll have the grounds. Non-consummation of our marriage will get you an annulment at the very least.'

'Really?' He looked at her, his eyes flint-hard. 'You know, my sweet, all that came remarkably neatly off your tongue. I wonder——'

He seized her by the hair and, ignoring her cry of pain, turned her face to the light to study it, his lips pursed in a thin line. Lori's heart almost stopped beating. If Alex, ruthless, unscrupulous swine that he was, once suspected the plot, he would destroy James and keep her prisoner for ever, for the sheer vindictive pleasure of completing his vendetta.

Somehow, she managed to return his gaze impassively until, as though satisfied, he finally released his grip, his hands sliding instead to the sides of her throat.

'Such a beautiful neck,' he remarked, his fingers stroking over the soft skin, 'such a beautiful face, hair—and——'

With one hand, he tore open the négligé, so that she heard the ribbons burst apart, then, before she could do more than give a terrified whimper, he caught hold of the low-cut lace bodice of her matching nightie and effortlessly ripped it apart.

'—and,' his voice deepened huskily, 'such a beautiful body. No one, I'm sure, would blame me if I were to take you—right now.'

'Y-you wouldn't do that.' As she lay helpless, stark terror engulfed her so that she could barely whisper.

He gave her, not that sleek cat's smile, but the smile of a predatory panther. 'Wouldn't I?'

'No,' she said desperately. 'You're far too proud to demean yourself.'

'You think so? Let's see, shall we?'

She saw the sudden intent in his eyes, but before she could react he lifted her bodily into his arms, holding her to him, his fingers splayed against her jaw as he savagely plundered her mouth.

Sobbing for breath, she wrestled with him, writhing in his grasp, thrusting her naked body heedlessly against that terrifyingly hard masculine frame, in a frantic effort to break his hold. Her struggles, though, had no more effect than would a terrified wren fluttering in his imprisoning fingers, beating its wings helplessly.

Her breath was thundering in her ears so that she was afraid she would faint. But then, miraculously, she wrenched her mouth free for an instant, and sank her teeth into his shoulder. With a furious oath, he flung her from him so that she lay sprawled on the bed. As he looked down at his shoulder, Lori put a hand to her mouth in horror for, through a haze of tears, she saw the distinct double set of bluish teeth marks, tiny beads of blood already oozing through the skin.

Terror—and shame—coursing through her, she went to slide off the bed, but he was too quick for her.

'Come here, you,' he snarled.

Pouncing on her, he seized her round the waist and dragged her back across the bed. One hand pinned her arms above her head while with the other he ripped away the last shreds of her ruined nightdress. Then, putting his hand to the belt of his wrap, he tore it open. Ignoring her stifled cry of terror, he moved across her, thrust apart her legs with his knee, and she felt him, hard and fiercely demanding, against her inner thighs. She closed her eyes, as a last despairing little whimper broke from her.

Next moment, though, as she tensed, helplessly waiting for the savage thrust that must splinter the world around her ears for ever, he rolled away from her.

'Cover yourself up.' He was drawing harsh, deep breaths into his lungs.

He tossed her négligé at her, and as she fumbled herself into it, her hands shaking so much that she could scarcely hold the flimsy silk, he went on, his voice thick with distaste, 'You're quite right. I will not rape any woman.'

'N-not even your wife?'

'Especially not my wife.' He paused, impaling her with his wintry grey eyes. 'I'll just tell you this—I fully intend to have an heir to the precious Baresi empire, as you so charmingly put it. And I also intend that you will provide it.'

After the ice-cold shock, merciful anger came flooding back. 'Never! I've told you——'

'And I promise you this. You may, for whatever twisted reason, think you've embarked on a life of celibacy, but sooner or later you will crawl to me on your knees, begging me for it. Then, and only then, will we make love.'

Somehow she gathered up the tattered rags of her defiance. 'Well, that's fine, then, because I shan't—ever.'

Leaning forward, he brushed the flat of his hand across her breasts and, incredulously, Lori felt the immediate response, the leaping of blood engorging the nipples, making them press urgently against the cobweb silk.

'No?' Alex smiled, but there was no humour in the thin smile. Then, getting up with cool deliberation, he shed his robe so that he stood before her, quite naked.

'W-what are you doing?'

'Oh, don't be alarmed, my sweet,' he sneered. 'I'm coming to bed—to sleep.' And, pulling back the top coverlet, he slid between the sheets. 'Just one more thing. You stay here, in this bed beside me, or——'

He let the threat hang in the air between them, unfinished, then turned on his side away from her, and within a few minutes Lori heard his light, regular breathing as he dropped catlike into sleep. She listened for a long time, frozen where she still half sat, half lay, but then at last she switched off the lights and slipped into the extreme edge of the bed.

She ought to be over the moon, brimming with triumph. She'd won the first round, and that meant she was going to win the war. This time had been the hardest, but Alex, despite his threats, had accepted the truth of their marriage, and from now on it could only be easier—until he finally acknowledged the inevitable and let her go. But in that case, why were her cheeks wet with tears?

Through the long hours that she lay awake, over and over again she repeated to herself the mantra of James's name. And as she said it, she tried despairingly to conjure up his face, as it had appeared to her in that fleeting vision outside the church. But this time it was no use. She couldn't see James any more. Her mind—and her whole body—bore the imprint of only one man—Alex Baresi.

CHAPTER EIGHT

WHEN Lori roused next morning, Alex wasn't there. She rolled over lazily, without remembering, then remembered everything and immediately tensed up. But the other half of the bed was empty, and when she put a tentative hand out, laying it on the indentation in the pillow where his dark head had rested, it was quite cold.

Pushing back the bedclothes, she went listlessly through to the marble and gold bathroom, stripped off the wreckage of the beautiful silk nightdress and surveyed herself dispassionately in the full-length mirror.

Her face was paper-white except where black smudges had been brushed with a heavy hand beneath her green eyes, which in turn had taken on a fixed, blank expression. Her mouth twisted suddenly, painfully. If Alex saw her just at this moment, he certainly wouldn't want her—not the way he had last night.

There was a bluish bruise on one of her breasts, another on her inner thigh... Alex had so nearly taken her, as he'd threatened. But that final thrust had never come. Instead, he had pushed her away, that look of sick disgust for her contorting his face. A long, shuddering sigh racked her slim frame, then, slowly straightening up, she stepped into the shower cubicle.

When she went back through to the bedroom, it felt airless. Crossing to the windows, she pushed them open then stood, her hand still on the catch.

Almost directly beneath her, set among the formally laid-out gardens, she could see the swimming pool, just one solitary figure in it. Alex, scything his way up and down, punishing the blue-green water, his tanned, muscular shoulders cleaving through it. Each time, as he reached the end, he jack-knifed down, surfacing yards out to begin another rapid length. Even at this distance she could feel the pent-up anger emanating from that powerful body as he hurled himself into the physical activity.

Lori lingered, quite unable to drag herself away, her eyes fixed hypnotically on those rhythmic shoulders. Finally, he hauled himself out and stood, his dark hair plastered to his skull, rivulets of water running off his brown skin, sleek as some sea creature. He was quite naked, apart from minuscule black trunks which rode low on his hips, and as she stared down at him very strange sensations began building inside her.

There was a peculiar, churning feeling in the pit of her belly, not exactly unpleasant but deeply perturbing. Her hands felt clammy, and her lungs were being caught up in a pair of giant hands and viciously squeezed, so that she could scarcely draw a breath. What on earth was wrong with her? Was she ill—a virus, perhaps?

She shook her head in a vain attempt to clear the dizziness, and saw Alex roughly towelling himself. And at that same instant the scales fell from her eyes. Her throat made a strangled sound, half groan, half terrified sob. She wanted Alex. But it was impossible, utterly impossible. She hated, loathed everything about him, didn't she? So—how could she possibly feel this way?

She clung on to the window-frame, staring blankly at the pool, its surface still lapping softly where he'd disturbed it. Her brain, overwrought after the traumas of last night, was playing some dreadful trick on her. That was all it was, wasn't it?

But no—it was no use. Her body had finally taken hold of her mind, shaken it and shown her the humiliating, terrible truth. She desired Alex—desperately, hungrily.

'No, I don't,' she cried aloud, and banged her fists down hard on the sill, but her inner self merely mocked her pitiful attempts at self-deception.

Alex had disappeared. Only a trail of footprints led out of her line of vision. He was on his way back up here! But she couldn't meet him like this, not until she had her emotions well under control. Snatching up the turquoise shift dress in fine lawn which she had laid on the bed, she dragged it down over her head, thrust her arms into the sleeves so that the seams creaked, then leapt through to the bathroom.

She pulled a comb through her hair, trying not to see the so-different face which stared out at her—the treacherous flush on her cheeks and neck, the intense glitter of her eyes. Then she ran back through the bedroom, flung open the door, and came face to face with Alex.

A towel was slung around his neck, his hair was still damp, his skin gleaming, and all at once she felt an almost overwhelming desire to reach out and touch those glossy shoulders or run her fingers through the tiny, glistening curls across his chest.

'Going somewhere?' His voice was flat and expressionless, yet in this new awareness of him it cut her to the bone.

'N-no,' she stammered, and backed into the room, dropping her eyes so that they should not betray her.

Further along the corridor lift doors opened and a waiter appeared, wheeling a loaded breakfast-trolley. Alex gave a strange little grimace, then gestured him past them. As the waiter turned back, he saw the tray with the champagne, which he'd brought to their suite and opened with a flourish the moment they'd arrived the previous night.

The bottle, now awash with melted ice cubes, still sat forlornly in its silver bucket, but as he went to pick it up Alex, his voice crackling with impatience, said, 'Leave it, please,' and the man, obviously aware of the invisible tensions swirling around his head, hastily retreated.

As she watched, Alex picked up the bottle by the neck. 'The party's over, I think,' he remarked grimly, and went through to the bathroom from where, a moment later, she heard the Dom Perignon gurgling away.

When he came back, he walked past her to the wardrobe, pulling out a shirt and trousers, apparently at random. All the time, he wasn't quite looking at her, she noticed that.

'I'm going to shower. Start without me.'

He could have been speaking to someone he'd never met before. His voice was still utterly devoid of any emotion—no warmth, certainly, but no coldness either—and Lori would almost have welcomed his usual sardonic tone—anything rather than this new aloof, tight-lipped Alex.

All at once, her legs began to buckle under her and she sank down into an armchair, resting her head wearily on her hand. Oh, God, what a mess, what an awful, awful mess. These new, totally unexpected feelings for Alex didn't make any difference, of course. She was still fully determined to hold out against him. But raging sexual desire was a complication she could have done very well without. She was only thankful that her emotions had waited until this morning before erupting like this, or she would never have resisted him . . .

Rousing herself, she pulled the trolley towards her and, with a slightly shaky hand, poured out two cups of coffee.

When Alex emerged, he was in a white shirt and straight grey canvas jeans which hugged his hips and thighs in an almost indecent intimacy. As he crossed the carpet towards her, she felt her eyes drawn involuntarily to that central part of his anatomy, and tore them angrily away.

Throwing himself down into a chair, he snatched up his cup and took a gulp. He grimaced and set it down again, slopping some into the saucer.

'It's cold. Why the hell did you pour it?'

Her hands clenched in her lap, but all she allowed herself to say was, 'I'm sorry. You were longer than I expected. I'll get you another.'

'Don't bother. I can do it myself.'

Leaping to his feet he took the cup, hurled its contents down the bathroom basin then poured himself some more. But that too failed to please, judging from his scowl.

'Orange juice?'

'What?' Interrupted in morosely flicking his spoon against his saucer, he favoured her with another scowl. 'No, thanks.'

Reaching across for a croissant, he buttered it and began eating.

As Lori stretched forward for the silver coffee-pot he did the same, their hands met and instantly she drew back. He must have seen the reflex action for his brows came down, but his lips only tightened into that taut line again and he made no comment.

The silence was shrieking at her, until she felt that if it went on for another second she'd leap to her feet, up-end the trolley all over the deep-pile of the carpet and start screaming. Hastily, she went to speak, but her mouth was dry as desert sand.

'What?' He glanced up from a scrutiny of the pattern on his plate.

'I——' She ran the tip of her tongue round her lips. 'I was wondering what we were doing today.'

'I'm playing tennis all morning.'

'Oh.' She thought he might ask her if she wanted to play. Not that she would, of course—but he didn't.

'I—I thought perhaps you might want to leave—early, I mean,' she floundered through his silence.

'Because there's nothing to keep me here, you mean.' For the first time that morning, he raised his eyes and looked at her directly, so that her own fell in confusion. 'Of course we're not leaving. I said we're staying here for three days, and that's exactly what we're doing.' He glanced at his watch, then pushed back his chair. 'Lunch is at one. I'll see you then.'

When he'd gone, Lori stayed where she was, sipping lukewarm coffee which she barely tasted, until the waiter's discreet knock roused her once more.

Downstairs, she wandered around the public rooms until, in the lounge, she found a good range of books, several of them in English. She chose an Agatha Christie and settled herself on a shady seat in the garden. But it was no use. Not even *Murder on the Orient Express* could keep her thoughts away from the tennis court, and every so often, drawn towards it like a moth to a flame, she would watch, hidden by shrubs, as Alex, serving ace after venomous ace, pounded a series of unfortunate opponents into the dust.

And the next two days passed in that way, Alex swimming, playing endless games of tennis, so that they

met only for meals, when the strain of keeping up the
flow of brittle, empty conversation was almost more than
she could bear. More than once, as she felt a lump rise
in her throat, she had to lower her eyes to her plate as
she struggled to control herself once more.

After that first terrible morning, she never allowed
herself really to look at him. She tried telling herself,
over and over, that it was just a moment of madness,
that she didn't really feel that way about him, but it was
no use. Whenever he was away from her, her body
yearned for him; and whenever he was near her she ached
to reach out and touch him.

The nights were worst of all, lying awake with that
marvellous naked body seemingly relaxed in sleep inches
away from her. But Alex made no move towards her,
and barely seemed to notice that she was there.

'Oh, I—I'm sorry.' Lori brought herself up sharply in
the doorway of Alex's office in the *palazzo*, at the sight
of him in his shirt-sleeves, bent over his desk. 'I thought
you'd gone,' she added lamely.

For a moment, she felt his irritation at being disturbed by her, but then, 'Please,' he beckoned with a
peremptory hand, 'don't let me frighten you away.' So,
ignoring the caustic irony in his tone, she advanced into
the room.

The last couple of weeks, he'd kept away from her
whenever possible—and not only avoided being in the
same room, even though he continued to insist that they
share the same bed, but backed off from the slightest
physical contact with her. And she was glad, for only
when he wasn't there, in the flesh, was it possible for
her to hold on to her turbulent feelings.

'Perhaps you'd like to see these?'

She winced at the chill formality, but obediently went over to the desk. Scattered over it were papers, architectural drawings, and photographs of an old house, in various stages of renovation. She looked enquiringly up at him.

'I bought this place last year as a country home—or rather,' he added wryly, 'a bolt-hole to escape to.'

'Oh—I didn't know.'

He shrugged. 'How should you?' Picking out one of the photographs, he held it out to her. 'This is the first one I took, the day I bought it.'

'But it was a complete ruin.'

The faintest smile cracked his taut face for an instant. 'Almost. That's why I bought it. I'm doing most of the work myself, when I can get out there.'

'I see.' She marvelled inwardly at the sheer animal energy of the man.

He indicated another photograph on the desk. 'In this one I've almost got the roof on—with just a little help from the local roofing experts, of course.' He smiled deprecatingly.

'Is it near here?'

'Good heavens, no. It's on the lower slopes of the Euganean Hills. Come round here—I'll show you.' On the wall behind the desk was a framed map of the Veneto. 'There's Padua. Follow this road—here—see that village?'

'Y-yes.' The word came out very oddly. She was standing so close to him that she could smell his spicy aftershave and, beneath it, the intoxicating smell that was Alex. Did every man's body smell so masculine, so seductively enticing? No, of course not. James's didn't—— Horrified, she caught herself up, dragging her attention back to the map.

'There's just this one road heading west out of the village. And it leads directly to my house—here.'

His breath was warm on her cheek, his pointing hand inches away from her face. Supple, strong, beautiful—for a fleeting second she saw it, deeply tanned, against her own pale skin, and stepped back abruptly.

'It looks very nice,' she said inadequately, and turned to the desk. 'This photo—it must have been taken in spring.'

'Yes, earlier this year. It looks its best then, I think— the fruit trees in blossom in the orchard, the wild flowers out in the meadows all round it.'

The beauty of the scene Alex was conjuring up brought sudden tears stinging her eyes. 'I—I'd love to see it,' she said hesitantly.

She wasn't looking at him, but she felt the slight pause and braced herself for a blank refusal; then he said, 'Perhaps I'll take you with me—some time.'

'And maybe, well—perhaps I could help you—with the inside.' It came out in a rush. How crazy could you get? She wasn't going to be here by the time he reached that stage, was she?

But in any case, Alex replied coolly, 'I don't think that would be a very good idea.'

'Oh.' He was quite right, of course, but all the same she felt as though he'd slapped her across the face. More and more, she was feeling excluded from his life, and that was precisely what he intended. Her punishment for defying him. How he must hate her—and, in that case, surely he'd be more than happy to end this appalling farce of a marriage just as soon as he possibly could. In which case, why was she——?

Beside them, the telephone rang and Alex snatched it up.

'Baresi,' he snapped, but then the irritated tone vanished. 'Giulia!' Exclamations, then a torrent of Italian before finally he replaced the receiver.

'A minor crisis at the works. I must go—I should be there already.'

Beside the map a wall safe stood open. He was snatching papers out of it as he spoke and cramming them into his attaché case. He slammed the safe to, clicking the combination dials and giving them a final tug. Glancing over his shoulder, he saw her watching him and smiled wryly.

'Can't be too careful these days.'

'No,' replied Lori, then, before she could stop herself, she went on very evenly, 'especially with a thief in the house.'

He paused in the act of snatching up his jacket, eyeing her narrowly, but then his lips twisted slightly and he said, 'How right you are.'

She stood stock still, feeling the anguish wash through her. A thief—and a cheat in the marriage bed. That was how he saw her. Surely, surely he'd want to be rid of her just as fast as he possibly could, and then this dreadful half-life would be over.

In the doorway, he looked back at her briefly. 'I'll be late again tonight. I've already told Olga not to prepare dinner for me.'

Ever since they'd got to the *palazzo*, this had been the pattern, with Alex either spending his evenings working down here, or not coming back at all until she was already in bed. Was it really work which detained him? she asked herself suddenly. Or was he already finding consolation elsewhere? After all, he'd told her clearly enough that that was the way it would be...

Sinking down into his leather chair, she propped her head on one hand and stared listlessly down at the pile of photographs. In one, a rather unkempt-looking black and white cat was patting at a rotten apple. Probably a stray. Maybe Alex fed it when he was there, but otherwise—unwanted. She bit her lip as a flood of tears threatened to drown her. Oh, for goodness' sake—crying for a cat you've never even seen? she mocked herself savagely.

She tidied the photographs away into the manila folder, straightened Alex's pens and pencils, then sat back wearily. Another endless day to be dragged through, either here in the *palazzo*, or more likely these days, as she became increasingly aware of the curious glances from the staff, wandering through the endless maze of little alleys and *piazzas*, over humpy wrought-iron bridges and among the criss-cross canals. She kept away from the San Marco area—everyone there always seemed to be having such a good time. Tourist parties, smaller groups, couples entwined in each other's arms—Venice seemed full of lovers, and she was always alone.

Only this morning, she'd thought of ringing Giulia to suggest they spend the day together—shopping, lunch in town—but that phone call just now had sharply reminded her. Giulia worked at the family glassworks, a highly valued member of the team, no doubt. A designer, wasn't she? Alex's right-hand girl. Lori's face twisted up suddenly as though she was in pain and, pushing back her chair, she went quickly out of the room...

A couple of afternoons later, bored almost out of her mind, she made her way rather nervously to the kitchen, where Olga Cerezo ruled her stainless steel and grey melanine kingdom with a rod of iron.

'Signora Cerezo, *per favore*,' she began, then went on stumblingly, the words carefully culled from her Italian phrasebook. 'I've never learnt to cook Italian dishes and I wonder if you'd teach me.'

The woman hesitated for a moment then smiled, put her in an apron and they set to work...

That evening, for once, Alex was back early. As usual he disappeared into his office, but emerged in time for dinner. The first course—tagliatelle with cream and fresh herbs—was brought in by the maid. Alex helped himself absently and began eating, moodily twirling the thin strands with his fork. Gradually, though, he must have become aware of her eyes on him, for he glanced up.

'Is something wrong?' That formal politeness again, which cut her in two.

'N-no. Er—do you like it?'

'Why?'

'Well—I made it.'

'It's fine,' he said briefly.

'No, it isn't.' She flung down her fork. 'You don't like it.'

He muttered something under his breath, then, 'Did I say I didn't like the bloody stuff?'

'You didn't have to. Don't worry, I won't bother——'

'Oh, for——' Tight-lipped, he got to his feet, wiped his mouth and hurled down the napkin, then pushed back his chair so that it tottered and fell.

'W-where are you going?'

'Out. I suddenly find I'm not hungry.'

* * *

Lori opened the front door and let herself in quietly
What a relief to be in the cool, dim hall after the ove
which was Venice. Even with her hair piled up into
knot—she hadn't yet summoned the courage to have
cut—her neck felt hot and sticky.

She put her hand on the banister, meaning to go up
and shower, then hesitated. A swim would be wonderful. Until now, she'd resolutely kept away from Alex's
pool, terrified she'd meet him there, his superb body
clad only in those lethal trunks—or less. But today there
was no danger. He'd told her he'd be late—again.

Running up to fetch her aquamarine Lycra bikini, she
opened the basement door and switched on the lights
so that the pool sprang into blue-green life. The wat
was cool as satin against her hot skin and she swam lazil
for a long time, revelling in the feel of it, for once th
litany of unhappy thoughts which her brain seemed to
recite non-stop these days blotted out.

And then, without warning, the door opened and Alex
appeared, still in his pale grey business suit. She wa
down at the shallow end, obscured from view by th
bank of potted plants, and he obviously did not see he.
as he stood, shrugging off his lightweight jacket.

He looked tired—very tired. So often these days she
avoided looking directly at him, but now she was shocke
to see how utterly drained he seemed, the lines of strain
round his eyes and mouth biting deep. All at once, before
she could put back in place the crucial safety-catch on
her mind, she longed to take him in her arms and kiss
that tension from his face.

At the shocking thought, her body moved involuntarily and though it made only the faintest ripple in the
water, Alex caught it. He glanced down swiftly at her,

his eyes hooding, his face drawing over itself its habitual aloof expression.

'Sorry. I didn't know you were here.'

As he half turned away, she began climbing up the tiled steps towards him.

'No, please. Don't go. I—I've had my swim and you—well, you look as though you could do with one.' She smiled faintly up at him, but he only looked at her as if he didn't really see her. 'Please, Alex,' she added softly, and put her wet hand on his white shirt sleeve.

He stood gazing down at her, and she saw a tiny muscle working at the side of his mouth, then, 'No, I don't think so. It's almost dinnertime, after all.'

As the door closed behind him with a soft thud she stood quite still, her shoulders sagging. She'd deliberately set out to bring Alex's hatred down on her head, and she'd more than succeeded. Oh, why had she ever allowed herself to become involved in this horrible scheme? Was it possible to buy something—even something as priceless as the life of Paget's and her father's happiness—at too high a cost?

But then she set her shoulders once more. Not much longer, surely, Lori, she told herself, and then this whole terrible nightmare will be behind you. Very soon now you'll never have to face Alex's hatred, never even set eyes on him again—he'll send you away for ever. But strangely, there was no comfort in the thought. Rather, it caught painfully in her throat.

CHAPTER NINE

As LORI came downstairs to breakfast next morning, Alex emerged from his office. He grunted a 'Good morning,' but then, as she stood aside to let him go past her, he said abruptly, 'The party next week, it's fancy dress of course—and masked.'

'What party?' She looked at him in bewilderment.

'Next Thursday. Your birthday party, of course,' as she still gazed at him blankly.

'Oh.' Lori put a hand to her mouth—she'd completely forgotten. She'd been so preoccupied with her own unhappiness that her twenty-first birthday could have come and gone without her remembering—or caring.

'But I don't want a party,' she blurted out. The mere thought of having to rouse herself to be a vivacious and sparkling Birthday Girl curdled her stomach.

'Don't be a fool. Of course you're having a party.' Alex's voice gave the impression of extreme irritation, barely reined in. 'A masked ball for a twenty-first is the Baresi tradition.'

'Oh, to hell with the Baresi tradition!' Lori punched her hand down on the banister. 'I'm not a Baresi—and I never will be,' she added defiantly.

Alex's brows came down in a thunderous scowl. 'You are a Baresi—Signora Alessandro Baresi. Whether you like it or not.'

'Which I don't.'

'And, whether you like it or not, you are having a party. There is no need for you to do anything—Olga

128

has all the arrangements in hand, and she can give you the names of several fancy dress suppliers in town for you to choose your costume.'

'I don't want a costume,' she replied stubbornly. 'Maybe I'll just go in my old jeans and sweatshirt that you won't let me wear.'

'Dressed as an unkempt art student, you mean?' he responded unpleasantly.

'No, as Lori Paget—endangered species.' She was playing with fire—she knew it—but she couldn't stop.

His lips tightened. 'I see you are determined to try my patience——'

'What patience?'

'—as far as you dare. But it's time that you took a hold of your childish bad temper.'

'I like that. *My* bad temper?'

'Or I shall have to teach you, once and for——'

The telephone rang on the small table at the foot of the stairs and Alex hooked up the receiver with his finger.

'Baresi.' He listened, then repeated, 'Baresi,' scowled and slammed it down. 'No one there—the third time this week. There must be a fault on the line. I'll report it later.'

'What are you doing today?'

The question came out of its own accord, and he gave her a long look before replying coolly, 'I'll be over at the works all day. Why?'

'Oh.' She shrugged slightly. 'No reason.'

When he was gone, Lori leaned against the banister. Whatever had possessed her to goad him in that childish manner? Maybe it was the overwhelming desire to break through the chill hostility to get some sort—any sort of reaction out of him. But whatever the reason, it was heading her into highly dangerous ground, for Alex simply wasn't a man to like being crossed. Well, too bad, she thought defiantly—the more she provoked him, the quicker he'd want to be shot of her.

Even so, before leaving the house she obtained from Signora Cerezo the names and addresses of the fancy dress shops, although they stayed forgotten in her bag as she wandered aimlessly round the town. Finally, she found herself on the Fondamente Nuove and stood, gazing across the lagoon. That island out there, it must be Murano... at this very moment, Alex was there...

A group of tourists was boarding a *vaporetto* which had drawn up alongside her. Idly, she read the destination board: *'Circolare destra: San Michele, Murano.'*

It was already moving away when she jumped on board and sat down on the slatted seat. Of course, he wouldn't be the least bit pleased to see her, she knew that. Her stomach lurched alarmingly at the thought of the reception she'd get. No, she'd just have a look round the island—maybe even visit one of the other glass-works— and Alex needn't even know she'd been across there...

'Posso aiutaria, signorina?' The young, smartly dressed woman looked up from behind her desk in the carpeted reception area.

Lori took a deep breath. *'Può indicarmi la direzione per——?'* she began haltingly.

The girl smiled. 'You are English?'

'Oh, yes,' said Lori gratefully. 'I—I'd like to see Signor Baresi, please.'

'I regret, *signorina*, that Signor Baresi is very busy this morning and he gave strict instructions that on no account is he to be disturbed.' The smile, though perfectly polite, was firm.

'I see,' Lori said slowly. She half turned away but then stopped. 'I'm sorry, but will you please tell him I'm here?'

'Well—what name is it?'

'Signora Baresi.'

The receptionist's jaw sagged very slightly, her glance flew to the wide gold band and that fabulous emerald ring which, no doubt, half of Venice was still talking about, but then she made an instant recovery. 'Of course. Please forgive me, *signora*.'

She had already put a finger on the intercom when Lori broke in urgently.

'No.' If he had the chance, he'd refuse point-blank to see her, and she couldn't bear that humiliation. 'If you'd just take me to his office, please.'

The girl hesitated a fraction—all Alex's staff were obviously terrorised into unquestioning obedience—then she stood up. 'But of course, *signora*. If you'll come with me.'

She pattered along a corridor in her high heels, then stopped at a door, smoothed back her immaculate chignon—Lori couldn't help noticing that—knocked briefly, opened it then gestured Lori in past her.

'Signora Baresi,' she said deferentially and fled, leaving Lori in the doorway, looking across at Alex and Giulia. They were standing together by the desk, their heads bent over some papers, so close that her softly curling brown hair swung against his shoulder.

They both looked up simultaneously, and she saw in Alex's face a mixture of surprise and exasperation, before it disappeared behind the mask of urbane politeness.

'*Cara*—how nice to see you. Come in.'

Crossing the room swiftly, he put his arm round her and kissed her cheek. They exchanged brief glances and his eyes shot her the warning—no one must suspect, least of all the family.

'Hello, Giulia.' Lori returned the other girl's smile, then went on, 'I—I had nothing else to do this morning, so I thought I'd come across.' She struggled to speak naturally. 'After all, I haven't been since—since the wedding. But if you're busy...' She tailed off uncertainly.

'Well, I think we've almost finished, haven't we, Giulia?' Alex glanced enquiringly at the girl and she nodded. 'So if you'd like to sit over there, I won't be long.'

So, like an obedient child, she perched on a chair while they continued their discussion, instantly, it seemed, forgetting her presence. She was excluded totally—it was as if the desk was a barrier, with them on one side, her on the other. If things had been different, she could have been standing there with them, or maybe just she and Alex, totally involved, working side by side...

It was Giulia who, in the end, at least made an effort to involve her. 'We're trying to develop a new technique for *pâte de verre* work, to make it more reliable in commercial production.'

'Oh, yes. We've had problems with that, too.' In her gratitude to Giulia, she was babbling. 'We've tried various formulae, but it's still so liable to shatter at the crucial stage, isn't it?'

Getting to her feet, she came towards the desk, but even as she did so Alex reached across and turned the papers over. It was an unobtrusive, seemingly negligent action but it stopped her dead in her tracks. He didn't trust her. But then, why should he? He'd be a fool to let her—a spy, an unscrupulous little sneak thief—come within a million miles of any top-secret papers ever again.

Giulia, though, did not seem to have noticed the gesture, so Lori somehow fought back her half-angry, half-anguished response and stood watching as she began gathering up the papers. As she did so, Alex put his arm lightly round her shoulders and dropped a kiss on her nose. And instantly, the ugly green flower of jealousy blossomed inside Lori's guts, so that she had to jam her hands into the pockets of her cream silk suit against the urge to seize the innocent, totally harmless Giulia and tear her apart.

For a few moments, struggling for composure, she missed their conversation, and came to to hear Alex say teasingly, 'And what's this I hear about a new boyfriend?'

Lori heard the girl give a faint, horrified gasp, then she coloured deeply. 'H-how did you know?'

'Ah, a little bird.' Alex shook his head mysteriously, then obviously relented. 'Silvia told me. Well, little one, when are we to be allowed to meet this paragon?'

'Oh,' Giulia was blushing scarlet. 'Well—I don't know.'

'He's a Venetian, I trust?' He was still teasing her.

'No—at least, he works in Venice.'

Alex patted her cheek fondly. 'Well, I shall expect to give him the once-over very soon.'

As Giulia gathered up her things and scuttled out, Lori watched her, the jealousy still seething inside her. It was obvious that Alex had nothing but cousinly feelings for the girl. And yet—he shouldn't show that easy affection for *any* woman, she thought resentfully. Only for you, a little inner voice whispered in her ear and, horrified, she took a step back, away from him.

Alex looked across the desk at her, all the affection frozen off his face. 'I'm going into the works. Are you coming?'

It wasn't exactly a warm invitation—no arm on her shoulder, no *'cara'* now they were alone—but it would keep her with him for a little while longer.

She shrugged her shoulders with a show of carelessness. 'I may as well. I've nothing better to do.'

He led the way further along the corridor, opened double doors and instantly they moved from an air-conditioned world of deep-pile carpets, show cases and potted plants into an inferno of noise and heat.

She'd been no more than a babe in arms when her father first took her to Paget's. Now, she smiled involuntarily as her nostrils inhaled the familiar acrid smell, and the sheer pleasure of being back in a glass-works swept through her. It was something she'd never got used to, that out of this noise and dust and filth, from a heap of sand, soda and lime, and the skill of a man's hands, came creations of marvellous, delicate beauty.

All round her, men were working in teams of four, stripped to the waist, outlined against the mouths of small, glowing furnaces. A middle-aged man, his face shiny with sweat, straightened up and said something to Alex. He responded with a nod, then turned to her, grimacing slightly.

'You've timed your visit well. Giuseppe says the glass I asked him to prepare is ready for me.'

'But I thought you said you never do any these days.'

'I don't normally. This is—different.'

She looked round the workshop floor. 'Who are you working with?'

'This is a one-man job.' He was looking at her steadily. 'I have to do it alone.'

'You mean——?' She stared up at him, shocked out of her brittle composure.

'Precisely.' An ironic smile quirked his lips. 'Your wedding present.'

'But you can't. I don't want you to.'

'I told you, my sweet. It is the duty of all Baresi husbands to make a gift for their loving brides.'

'Well, in our case, then, there's no need, is there?' She was trying desperately to fight down the hysteria that was all but taking her over. A masked ball for her twenty-first birthday, and now this—Alex grimly determined to stick to all the expected trappings of a happy Baresi marriage.

'There is every need,' he said tightly. 'Apart from anything else, it is supposed to be a test of the husband's prowess—in glass blowing,' he added, after the faintest of pauses.

'But I'm sure I'm not supposed to watch.'

'It's not usual, no. But you're here now, and everything is prepared.'

'Please, Alex,' she whispered frantically. 'I—I'd far rather you didn't.'

'But we mustn't disappoint the work-force, must we?' Her gaze went to the groups of men, glancing up from their tasks to eye them both curiously. 'They're very eager, no doubt, to see what I can produce for my beautiful English bride,' he added, a glint of cold mockery in his grey eyes.

'W-what are you going to make, then?' A bowl, or a dish, like the first Alessandro's—please let it be something as meaningless as that.

'A loving cup. That's the most suitable thing, I think, don't you?'

And he turned away, shrugging himself out of his jacket. He passed it to her, followed by his tie, then his shirt. She could feel the warmth of his flesh on it still and swallowed, desperately keeping her eyes away from that magnificent torso.

Backing up against the grimy wall, well out of the way, she watched as he methodically checked the tools on the bench then took up one of the long iron rods. He was frowning slightly and, tuned in on his wavelength, she could feel the tension in him—this first moment was always nerve-tingling, she knew that herself. But then, as he turned towards the furnace, she also knew that now he would have excluded her and everything around him, and have fixed his mind in utter concentration.

Giuseppe slid open the furnace door and Alex thrust the end of the rod into its red-gold heart, twirling it slowly round and round between his hands. Then, gradually he withdrew it, the gathered liquid fluid and glowing, like a living thing. He rolled it slowly on the bench to cool it then, putting his mouth to the other end of the pipe, began to blow the glass into a molten bubble. Lori knew every moment of this most skilled operation—had done it herself a hundred times—yet she'd never watched with such intensity.

Alex was alternately blowing and shaping the fluid, returning to the furnace for more gathers of liquid glass, until his tanned skin was slicked with sweat and gleaming like sleek satin. Beneath the satin the muscles of his back and arms moved, in a finely balanced blend of strength and grace.

And suddenly Lori's pulse-beat quickened, the blood drummed in her ears, as she felt herself snatched up in a tidal wave of physical desire. His body, so strong yet so graceful—to be held in those arms, caressed by those hands... Her lungs were tightening, until she was almost suffocating.

Mercifully, Alex remained totally oblivious of her, his needle-sharp mind incapable, for once, of picking up her inner turmoil. At a brief nod, Giuseppe brought forward more molten glass for him to pour on to the bottom of the cup to form its pedestal base, then still more, to shape the slender, curving handles.

How beautiful it was. She'd always thought of Alex solely as a successful businessman. Now, as the light of the furnace played over the glass, she realised that he was a master craftsman.

At last, he seemed to be satisfied and, wiping the sweat from his brow with the back of his hand, he took up one of the files. Lori stopped breathing altogether. This point, when the finished creation had to be set free by snapping the glass stem which tethered it to the iron rod, was the trickiest of all—the moment of truth, her father called it. A wrong move and the loving cup—*her* loving cup—would be cracked through, and Alex would crush it and hurl the fragments back into the furnace to be remelted. And suddenly, desperately, she knew that, more than anything else she'd ever wanted, she wanted that loving cup.

Grasping the file like a dagger, he brought it down hard on the rod, and the cup rolled away on to the bench, intact and perfect. Giuseppe glanced across at her, pantomiming a gusty sigh of relief, and the other men broke into a little round of applause.

Then Alex, his face flushed, his black hair flopping over his forehead, turned and grinned at her, his eyes alight with triumph. And at that precise moment—that moment of truth—as she smiled back at him, she

thought, with a strange fluttering feeling in her stomach,
I love him.

Her foolish jealousy, her wanderings day after empty
day, her physical yearnings for him—why hadn't they
warned her what was happening? But I can't, she thought
despairingly, I can't love him. I'm not the kind of girl
who's for ever falling in and out of love—and I love
James.

But you don't love James, that inner voice said, cold
and clear. You've never loved him, not really—and suddenly she knew that it was true. And now that you do
know the truth, what are you going to do? You're
trapped between a man who despises you, and another
who'll be dreadfully hurt if you don't keep your word
to him . . .

Alex was coming towards her, something of his
triumph still in his face, so that all at once she yearned
to take it between her hands and kiss it. Instead, she
managed an almost natural smile though she couldn't
quite meet his eyes.

'Congratulations. It's beautiful,' she said stiltedly.

'So glad you like it.' He was responding instantly to
her apparent coolness. Taking his clothes, which she had
forgotten she was clutching, he went on, 'I'll leave
Giuseppe to put it in the *lehr*.' He paused fractionally.
'Are you planning on spending the rest of the day over
here?'

'N-no,' she said quickly. He obviously wanted her
gone, and she too had to be alone, to try to make sense
of the hurricane of emotions which was lashing her.

'Right. I need a shower.' He put a hand on her arm,
then gave her what no doubt appeared a warm, loving
kiss, but his lips barely grazed her cheek. *'Ciao, angelo*

mio.' Once again, only she caught the faintly caustic edge, and he was gone.

Back in Venice, Lori wandered dazedly round for hours, but finally ended up at the *palazzo*. Shutting herself in the bedroom, she paced endlessly up and down, until Signora Cerezo knocked to tell her that Elena, Alex's eldest sister, had called, so she was forced to pin a bright welcoming smile on her face and go down to pour tea and make polite conversation.

Elena was just leaving when Alex arrived. 'Elena, how good to see you.' He kissed her on the cheek. 'Are you staying to dinner?'

'Sorry, but I can't.' She was looking closely at her brother, lips pursed reprovingly. 'You're working too hard, Alex. And as for my new sister-in-law——' Lori, who had been standing numbly in the background, jumped slightly and hastily refixed her slipping smile '—what are you thinking of, letting her get so tired and pale-looking? Unless——' she gave them both a quick glance and Lori's stomach lurched with sudden apprehension at what was coming '—there's a little Alessandro on the way.'

Lori's hands clenched convulsively on one another, and she shot Alex a look of desperate appeal.

'That's it, isn't it?' Elena, oblivious of the sudden tension, was smiling delightedly. 'Oh, Mamma will be so happy. Since the wedding she's thought of nothing——'

'I'm sorry to disappoint you, Elena.' Alex's voice, smooth as silk, cut in on her joyful flow. He slid an arm round Lori, pressing her to him. 'But no little Alessandro, as you put it. At least, not quite yet, eh, *cara*?'

Tilting Lori's face to him, he kissed her lightly on the lips. She knew that he was doing it for her sake at least as much as his own, but all the same she was barely able to respond, as a crazy laugh welled up in her at the dreadful irony of it all.

As soon as they waved Elena off, he dropped his arm from her waist as if her body were made of molten glass, and picked up his attaché case.

'Our sales director's coming to dinner tonight.' His voice was clipped. 'There are several matters I want to discuss with him which will keep me up late, so I'll sleep in the guest-room.'

'Oh. But I won't mind if you——'

'And I'll be making an early start for Paris in the morning.'

'Paris? You didn't tell me.'

'Didn't I?' he said briefly. 'I've got several meetings lined up there, so I'll probably be away several days.'

Lori tried to say something, but her voice failed. Alex had half turned away, but he paused.

'Yes?'

'Oh, nothing. At least, are you going on your own?'

He frowned slightly. 'To Paris? Yes, of course—why?'

'Oh, no reason.'

Alex, please, don't look at me like that. I love you. Don't you understand—can't you see? I love you. But he had already walked away and shut his office door. And anyway she couldn't tell him—the words would stick in her throat...

Next morning, without even going downstairs, Lori knew that he'd left. She lay for a long time, but finally hunched herself up in bed, her arms clasped round her knees. It was beginning already—Alex putting a 'total exclusion zone' between them. Last night was the first time they hadn't shared a bed, and today he was off, without the slightest thought of whether she might want to go with him. It was all so dreadfully ironic—James's scheme was working out even more successfully than either of them had dared hope. Except that——

James! Among all her inner turmoil was the anguish of what she was going to do about him, loyally working away to free her. The thought sent a violent stab of guilt through her, and she bit her lip as tears of misery burned her eyes.

But she would have to tell him. Whatever happened between her and Alex—even if he sent her away for ever—she couldn't go back to James. He'd be terribly hurt, of course, but in the end it would be even more wrong of her to marry him, knowing that she didn't love him, and that she would never, in all her life, love anyone but Alex. She'd write to him—today—and hope that he'd understand—and forgive her.

And Alex. Was it too late? She could tell him, of course, just as soon as he came back. 'Alex,' she'd say, 'I've been so foolish...' But he might meet her words with that chilling indifference that was becoming second nature to him whenever she was around, and she couldn't bear that.

'Sooner or later you will crawl to me on your knees'... Was that the way? No. He would only despise her even more, repel her with icy contempt—or, even worse, casually take her, but with that same icy contempt... Was there no other way that she could show him? She gnawed on her underlip, and unseeingly her gaze wandered around the room.

But then abruptly it focused on the painting on the wall facing her... 'You know, Lorina, with those flowers in your hair, you look just like Boticelli's *Primavera*'...

Dared she? Her heart beat a rapid tattoo, as she stared at the beautiful figure in the painting. Then, leaping out of bed, she crossed to the telephone extension and skimmed rapidly through her list of numbers. Yes, here it was—Signorina Giannini, dressmaker. She drew a deep breath, then, with fingers that trembled slightly, began to dial.

CHAPTER TEN

LORI was sitting at the dressing-table, her head bent forward as she struggled with the zip, when a door banged and she heard rapid footsteps coming upstairs. Alex. At last he was back. Her stomach jolted with relief and then apprehension, and nervously she ran the tip of her tongue round her lips. How would he react?

Her hands stilled as the door flew open and he appeared. He'd taken off his jacket and tie, and one hand was already to his top shirt button. She was out of his direct line of vision so that at first he didn't see her. But then, for an instant, he stopped dead, before coming slowly across to stand just behind her, looking down at her reflected face.

'Hello, Alex,' she said softly. 'I—I thought you weren't going to make the party.'

'So did I.' Their eyes were still locked and she felt the colour creeping into her cheeks but couldn't look away. 'The flight from Prague was delayed.'

'Prague?' She stared at him.

'Olga gave you my message, didn't she?' He sounded abstracted, as though most of his mind was on something else.

'Yes, of course.'

In fact, when the housekeeper had passed on the brief, impersonal message from Alex's secretary that he was flying straight on from Paris to eastern Europe, she'd come upstairs and cried. He couldn't bear to be near

143

her, loathing her so much. She'd almost rung Signorina
Giannini to cancel her instructions.

He was standing quite still, yet she felt the tension
emanating from him. Perhaps he despised her pathetic
effort, but was trying to hide it. After all, it was her
birthday, and he couldn't be that cruel.

Taking a deep breath to quell the butterflies that were
fluttering wildly inside her, she smiled up at him, then
leaned forward, her lashes screening her eyes.

'C-could you do the zip up for me, please? The muslin's so fine, I'm afraid of ripping it.'

'Keep still.' She felt his fingers moving her hair aside
from her neck, then carefully easing up the zip.

'Signorina Giannini made it for me.' She wished her
voice was not so unsteady. 'She's made a good job of
it, don't you think?'

'Stand up, so that I can see it properly.' His own voice
was almost—but not quite—under control.

She got up slowly, so that the long flowing gown of
white flower-sprigged muslin fell to her bare ankles.

'I was lucky.' Still that slightly tremulous voice. 'She
had this material. It isn't exactly like *hers*—like in your
painting, I mean,' just in case he hadn't got the message,
'but it's very similar. And with my hair down like this,
and these rosebuds she brought to go in it, well, I——'

'Be quiet,' Alex said huskily and she knew, with
sudden joy, that he was seeing, not the fine fabric itself,
but the way it clung to her, emphasising her high breasts,
the lovely long line of her hip and thigh. He stood
looking down at her, his expression quite unreadable,
but along his cheekbones she saw the very faintest flush
of darker colour.

'It's lovely—the neckline.' Lifting his hand, he touched
the ruffled edging and, feeling his skin warm through

the flimsy material, she closed her eyes for an instant. 'It sets off your face—like a delicate flower.' And his hand brushed across her lips.

'Oh, Alex.' It was the faintest breath against his fingers, but it was enough.

With an incoherent exclamation, he pulled her roughly into his arms, and Lori, her whole being aching with the love which she had so yearned to show, put her arms around him, straining him to her. He buried his lips in the warm angle between her shoulder and throat, and her fingers twined in his dark hair as, alight with sensations she had hardly known existed till now, she arched her neck against him.

She heard him groan, then his fingers were on her neckline, pulling it down on to her shoulders, at the same time moulding one of her breasts through the muslin, pulling it up away from the dress, until the soft, rounded flesh was free. Against her nipple, his lips were hot, and they were setting her on fire too, as a scorching heat ran through her veins, setting every part of her body smouldering then bursting into flames.

'Signor Baresi.'

The housekeeper's voice, and then a soft, discreet knock at the door, making them leap apart. A choked gasp burst from Lori and, eyes dazed, she clung to Alex for support. Putting his hand gently over her mouth, he pulled her to him.

'What is it, Olga?' he called, his tone almost normal.

'I'm sorry, *signor*, but the first guests are arriving.'

A muttered curse, then, 'Make my—our apologies. We'll be down in five minutes.'

As the footsteps receded, he held Lori against him and gradually his heartbeat, which she could feel pounding against her ribs in tune with her own, steadied. Then he put her away from him and stood, one hand holding her by the wrist, the other tilting her face to him. His own face was flushed, a sensual little smile playing round his lips, and the expression in his eyes made her breath catch in her throat.

'S-so you approve of my choice of costume?' she managed to get out.

He inclined his head. 'Certainly.'

'And what about you? What are you wearing?'

'Ah, *piccola*.' He tapped her nose softly. 'Wait and see. But I must have a quick shower first.' And tearing off his shirt, he disappeared into the bathroom.

Moments later he was back, beads of water glinting in his hair, his skin still damp. She could see rather a lot of his skin—he was wearing only a small towel, slung round his hips and carelessly knotted. Their eyes met, Alex stood quite still, and for a moment the sexual tension throbbed in the air between them, then he said abruptly, 'My costume's in my dressing-room,' and he was gone again.

To try and quell the clamour of her blood, Lori began fidgeting with the rosebuds in her hair. She had just replaced the final one, in exactly the same place, when Alex yelled, 'Lori—come in here.'

When she opened the door, he was standing in front of the mirror, his hands to his throat, where a white lace ruffle hung lop-sidedly. He turned and scowled at her. 'I can't do this bloody thing up.'

'Here, let me,' she said soothingly and, putting his hands out of the way, tweaked the beautiful lace this way and that, while Alex fulminated under his breath. Finally, she gave it a pat and stood back. 'I think that's all right.'

'Thanks.' He flashed her an apologetic grin then, snatching up a black, shawl-collared cloak, he swirled it over his shoulder. 'Well, how do I look, then?'

'You look—very nice,' Lori said, through a strange breathlessness. Skin-tight pale grey breeches, black knee-high boots, a white lace-edged shirt, the ruffle at his neck setting off his strong throat.

She smiled rather shyly at him. 'You know, I think you were born two centuries too late. You should always wear eighteenth-century costume.'

He put back his head and laughed, his white teeth gleaming. 'But I wouldn't have known you then, would I? So you like me as a prototype corporate raider, do you?'

'A what?'

He turned away for a moment, put something to his face and when he swung back he was wearing a black mask. From a leather case, he took a pair of silver-handled pistols, spun them round then levelled them at her.

'Don't worry, *cara*,' as she gave an involuntary gasp. 'They're not loaded.'

Light dawned. 'You're a *highwayman*!'

'Of course.' An even more wicked grin. 'I seem to rememb⸆r you telling me once how fitting it would be.' He swept her a low bow. 'Ready?'

'Oh, let me just put my mask on.' She pulled on the narrow slip of black velvet.

'But aren't you wearing shoes?'

She shook her head decidedly. 'No. Primavera doesn't wear shoes, not for running through the meadows.'

'But, *angelo mio*,' his voice dropped to a murmur, 'don't you know what happens to young girls who run through the meadows barefoot?'

'Tell me.' She gave him an innocent, wide-eyed look, and he smiled a slow, secret smile that made her heartbeat quicken again.

'I think it would be far better to show you.' Gently easing up her neckline, he ran the tips of his fingers just once along the very edge of the ruffles, so that her skin tingled. She swayed towards him, eyes closing, but he held her away from him.

'*No*, my sweet—or Olga will be in apoplexies downstairs. But when our guests have gone,' that slow smile again, 'then the rest of your birthday night is ours.'

Fingers intertwined, they went along the corridor and down the wide, sweeping staircase, to be greeted by the applauding guests.

'Lori, my child——' her mother-in-law clutched her to her bosom '—you look enchanting. Happy birthday.'

'Yes—happy birthday,' a hundred other voices chimed in, and, with the good wishes ringing in her ears, Alex led her through to the salon to open the dancing.

Over the next couple of hours she was claimed by first one then another partner, but although she spent very little time at Alex's side, and smiled and laughed and blushed prettily at all the compliments, with every fibre of her being, for every second, she was conscious of him, some sixth sense telling her exactly where he was, so that every few minutes their eyes would meet across the room and they would exchange a swift, secret look, full of promise of the night to come.

Yet another dance ended, her partner bowed, then, as she turned away, she found herself face to face with another man, in the costume of one of Garibaldi's freedom fighters. His mask was a three-quarter one so that, with the floppy hat pulled down low over his brow, his face was invisible.

As the music began again, without even a 'May I?' he took her in his arms, so with a polite smile she allowed herself to be waltzed down the room. When they reached the far end, though, he suddenly whirled her through the open double doors to the ante-room, then right out into the small patio-garden at the back of the *palazzo*.

'Where are you taking me?' She was laughing, but even so a slight prickle of unease tingled her spine. 'Who are you?'

Still without speaking, the man drew her back from the direct light which was streaming out, put his hand up to his face, peeled off his mask and turned to reveal the laughing face of——

'James!'

In an instant, all the laughter in her own face died and she went very pale, one hand to her throat.

'Hello, Lori.' He was grinning at her triumphantly, and she struggled to pull herself together.

'H-how—what are you doing here?' she whispered.

'Come to see my beautiful fiancée, of course. You surely didn't think I'd stay away from your twenty-first birthday party, did you?'

'I—I——' Her legs were almost giving way under her. She leaned up against a white wrought-iron chair for support.

'Clever James, eh?' He was so full of himself, his boyish features beaming with jubilation, that he didn't notice Lori's frozen stillness.

'But—how did you get in here? You haven't gate-crashed, have you?' Terror for him filled her. 'If Alex finds you——'

'No, of course I haven't gatecrashed. I've been invited.'

'Who by?'

He tapped the side of his nose and winked. 'Friends in high places, darling.'

Lori frowned in puzzlement. What on earth was he talking about? But there wasn't time—any moment, someone might appear.

'Er—James.' She swallowed. 'That letter——'

He must have come in response to it, to plead with her. In which case, she was going to have to hurt him even more, and her soft heart quailed at the thought.

'Letter? I haven't had a letter. Mind you, I've been out here for the last few weeks.'

'You mean you've been in *Venice*?' She gaped at him, horror-stricken. If Alex had seen him——

'Yes. I'm working out here—for Maldini.'

'Maldini?' She knew the name—another Murano-based glass firm.

'That's right. Very fitting, don't you think? That bastard throws me out of a job, so I get myself fixed up with his deadliest rivals. Look, Lori,' as a roll of drums signalled the end of another dance, 'that idea of mine about a management buy-out to regain Paget's—well, it's no go, I'm afraid. Baresi's already got his own people in all the key positions. The rest of the plan's still on, of course—about you and him, I mean——'

'James, I——'

'And there are other ways to get our own back on that swine.'

'W-what do you mean?'

'That husband of yours—you may not realise it but he's in danger of overstretching himself.'

'No, I didn't know that,' she said slowly.

'Paget's isn't the only firm he's taken over recently, and now he's trying to open up markets in eastern Europe.'

Lori stared at him. 'How on earth do you know that?'

'As I said, the right friends in the right places.'

She frowned in puzzlement. 'What are you talking about?'

But he only shook his head and smirked tantalisingly. She barely saw the smirk, though—her mind was in overdrive. James...working for Maldini... What had he said? Alex's deadliest rivals... She'd have to warn Alex, that was certain—but that would mean letting him know about James and her, wouldn't it?

'And when a man's in that situation, well——' And with the side of his hand, he mimed slitting his throat.

Lori shuddered inwardly. He was, she knew, only acting for the best, but even so——

'Er—what exactly are you doing with Maldini?'

James gave her a knowing look. 'Ask no questions, my sweet, and you'll be told no——' A gust of laughter came from the room behind them and he glanced swiftly over his shoulder. 'We haven't time now, but you'll know soon enough. Let's just say, you won't have to fight that swine off for very much longer. You've managed it so far?'

She coloured deeply. 'Y-yes, I have, but——'

'I've tried phoning to let you know I'm around, but every time I rang that bastard or some stupid woman answered so I put the receiver back down double quick.'

So all those faults on the line... Lori realised, with a start, that he was eyeing her closely.

'I must say, my sweet, married life—even to that devil—seems to suit you. You're looking very fetching tonight. Highly—desirable.' His voice was slurred slightly and, for the first time, she registered the smell of wine on his breath. 'Even more beautiful than on your wedding day.'

'You were *there*?' Her eyes almost swallowed up the rest of her face. 'In the square?'

'Of course.'

So she hadn't been hallucinating. Again, she felt rise in her the terror of what Alex would have done if he'd known.

'But—why?' Why give yourself unnecessary pain? she thought, but couldn't say it.

'Curiosity, I suppose. A sneak preview of our own wedding day.'

At last, from somewhere deep down, she found the strength to speak the words. 'James, please, don't go on. There's something I must tell you. I—I can't go through with it.'

His eyes narrowed slightly. 'What the hell do you mean?'

'I can't go through with it,' she repeated. 'Leave Alex and marry you, I mean.' She'd meant to put it so gently, as she'd tried to in her letter, but in the end maybe the pain for him would be less if she were to be brutal.

'What?'

'I'm so sorry, James.' She tried to take his hand but he shook himself free. 'But it would be wrong to marry you. You see, I don't love you. I know now that I love Alex.'

For a moment, there was utter silence, then, 'How romantic.' James's face twisted into a sneer, all the boyish good humour wiped clean. 'Well, well. It hasn't taken you long, has it?'

'W-what do you mean?'

'Love? Don't make me laugh. Money, that's what's got to you, my dear. All this.' He gestured behind him to the *palazzo*, vibrant with music and laughter. 'Glitz, glamour—and money.'

'*No.* Don't think I haven't asked myself that, over and over, but it isn't that, I swear it. Oh, James,' she was almost weeping, 'I'm so sorry.'

'Sorry!' His voice was tight with ill-concealed rage. 'You mean I've spent the last five years sucking up to that incompetent fool of a father of yours——'

'Oh!' Lori drew in a sharp gasp of horrified outrage.

'And as for you, you stupid little cow——' He broke off, struggling for the words.

She closed her eyes momentarily and a tear squeezed itself out. 'W-what about me?' she asked tremulously.

'You, my sweet, were my passport to wealth—at least as long as Paget's had any life left in them. And since then you've been my way of getting even with that swine for the way he humiliated me that day.'

'You mean,' she said in a tiny, muffled voice, 'you don't love me—you've never loved me?'

He gave a cruel, lacerating laugh. 'Love you? Good God, no. But even so——'

She saw the intent in his eyes and turned to run, but she was too late as, grabbing her, he swung her round into his arms, pinning her against his body.

'No, please, James—let me go,' she whispered frantically. Even now, she wouldn't allow herself to call for help and bring Alex's wrath down on his head.

'Let you go? Not until I've had a taste of this delectable body of yours.'

And pressing his mouth to hers to silence her, he put up a hand, clawing at her breast, so that through the thin muslin she felt the clamminess of his palm as his fingers kneaded at the rounded flesh, viciously squeezing it in a hideous parody of Alex's embrace a few hours earlier.

Everything was going black around her, she couldn't breathe—but then she heard James give a little grunt and, mercifully, he was releasing her. She opened her eyes and saw him staggering back, caught in Alex's grip.

'What the hell do you think you're doing to my wife?' Alex's voice shook with fury. 'Lori, are you all right?'

'Y-yes.' She was taking in shuddering gulps of the cool night air. 'But you mustn't——'

'Right, you—let's have a look at you.'

He swung James round towards the light, as though he were a sawdust-filled doll, then she heard his breath hiss in his throat. Just for a moment, he looked across at her as she leaned against the chair, shaking in every limb, the nausea churning inside her, then his right hand came back and he smashed his fist into James's unprotected face.

Somehow, she roused herself. In this mood of murderous rage, he would surely kill him. Pushing herself upright, she seized his arm.

'No—no! Alex—don't.'

For a moment, it seemed as though he would ignore her frantic pleas, but then, with a contemptuous gesture, he released his hold and James staggered back before folding up into the chair.

'Get up.' Even she had never heard Alex use quite that tone before. Remote, chill—and infinitely dangerous. 'Get up—and get out.'

James struggled to his feet and stood nursing his cut cheek, from which blood was oozing.

'You are a guest under my roof,' still that same voice, 'so I shall not touch you again. But if you ever enter this house again—and if you ever dare to lay a finger on my wife again—I swear I shall kill you with my bare hands.'

James half turned, then stopped, looking from Alex to Lori with an ugly expression on his once-handsome face. 'I'd watch that little wife of yours, if I were you, Baresi,' he said thickly. 'Don't think it was all me—she's hot for anything in trousers, that one.'

And then, even as Alex's fingers clenched at his side, he turned quickly away to disappear down a side passage.

She wanted Alex to turn to her, to take her into his arms, to soothe and comfort her. He did turn to her, very slowly, but then she saw behind the black mask the expression in his eyes.

'Cover yourself up.' Still that same voice, even though James had gone.

Looking down, she saw that in her frantic struggles her dress had been dragged down off one shoulder and one gleaming pearly breast was half exposed. With trembling fingers, she tugged the dress up.

'I didn't realise I had to vet your guest-list.'

'My——' Her fingers stilled. 'You don't think I invited James, do you?' Oh, God, he did. Stark terror had her by the throat. 'Please, Alex.'

'Please, Alex, what?'

'Please believe me.' Her body's terrible shaking was threatening to take her over completely.

'Believe you, you little——'

'So there you are.'

They both swung round, to see Elena in the doorway, clicking her tongue in reproof. 'Don't be greedy, brother dear. You can't keep Lori to yourself for the entire evening. At least, not till we've all gone.'

And she gave them a teasing smile, which all but made Lori burst into wild, hysterical peals of laughter. Then, oblivious to the jagged shards of tension which glittered

in the air all around them, she linked arms with them
both and drew them back into the house.

For the rest of the evening, whenever Lori sought and
found Alex in the crowded throng, his eyes were on her,
boring into her like chips of grey flint. And when, as
she blew out the candles on her magnificent pink-iced
cake and cut the first slice, his arm rested lightly on her
shoulders, the fingers were icy cold.

CHAPTER ELEVEN

'PRACTISING another seduction?'

Lori had been gazing fixedly into the dressing-table mirror at the stranger with the deathly pallor and haunted eyes. Now, she swung round to see Alex leaning against the door-jamb, watching her. Straightening up, he came into the room and softly closed the door.

He dropped his highwayman's cape on to the bed, followed by the pistols, then peeled off his mask, so that she could see even more clearly the frozen anger in his eyes.

She moistened her lips. 'Alex, I—I know how it must look, but do you really think I'd be so stupid as to invite James here? After all,' as his lip curled, goading her into some show of spirit, 'would I really dare to, knowing the way you might react?'

He shrugged. 'Where was the risk? A masked ball—an ideal set-up for an assignation with your lover.'

'No!' She banged her fist down in frustration!

'If only you could have kept your hands off each other,' his savage tone flayed the skin off her, 'no one would have been any the wiser.'

'No,' she repeated loudly, 'it wasn't like that. You must believe me. Someone invited him—he told me that—but I swear it wasn't me.'

'Who was it, then? My mother? Elena? Marcello?'

'Yes. No. Oh, I don't know.' She put her hands to her head. 'But I only know I didn't.'

'Oh, please.' His tone went down from chill to Arctic. 'Credit me with a little intelligence. After all——' another notch, from Arctic to glacial '—who but you here in Venice knows Forsyth? No one.'

She clutched at his words. 'But James told me that he knows somebody here. He—he's working for Maldini.'

'What?' Alex's face hardened even more, if that were possible.

'And—and he says that you're in danger of over-stretching yourself. Is that true?'

'A little, perhaps, but nothing I can't handle. Oh, don't worry, my sweet—your luxury lifestyle's not in any danger.'

'That's not what was worrying me, and you should know that,' she retorted hotly. 'But James has been out here for several weeks—ever since our wedding, in fact.'

Too late, she realised what she'd laid herself open to. She saw Alex's eyes narrow, then he crossed the room and stood over her, regarding her as she sat on the stool, and as his shadow fell across her she shivered.

'So, no wonder you've been able to resist my—fatal charm.' His lips thinned. 'All this time, you've had your lover to satisfy you.'

'I tell you, *no*.' This time, she snatched up her hairbrush and banged it down again, so that everything on the dressing-table rattled, then she looked up at him, her eyes very bright. 'Please, Alex, don't say these horrible things to me. One day, you'll be very sorry, I know.' Her voice trembled and she bit viciously on her soft inner lip. No power on earth would make her cry in front of him.

'Such innocence.' Bleakly, he studied her upturned face. 'But I don't think so. All your aimless drifting around Venice—you've been seeing him every day, no doubt. I've obviously underestimated that gentleman— he can't be such a cold fish, after all. Just a pity for you that I managed to get back here in time for the party— or by now you'd be celebrating your birthday together here, in this bed.'

'You're crazy. If you think I'd——'

'And that little scene up here, earlier. Any man would have done, wouldn't he? Well? Answer me,' as she stared blankly down at her hands, clasped in her lap, the fingers lacing and unlacing continuously. He caught hold of a handful of hair, wrenching her face up to his. 'Wouldn't he?'

'If you say so, Alex,' she muttered dully.

He stared into her face, then abruptly, as though afraid of what he might do, released her, shoving his hands into his pockets and going across to lean against the wall.

'Preferably Forsyth, but anyone—even your unfortunate husband.'

'Oh.' She put a hand to her mouth, flinching as if he really had struck her. But the biting contempt in his voice had roused her from her lethargy as nothing else could have done. Springing to her feet, she faced him across the no man's land of white carpet.

'You're quite determined to think the worst of me, Alex. Very well, I want to tell you something.'

'Please.' He shook his head wearily. 'No more lies.'

'No,' she replied, very clearly. 'It's precisely because I don't want any more lies that I'm going to tell you this.'

But her heart was beating very fast, as the enormity of the risk she was taking hit her. Angry and beyond reason as he already was, how would he react? But it was too late now to hold back.

'It started that day at Mallards—do you remember?'

He gave a brief, mirthless laugh. 'I'm hardly likely to have forgotten.'

'You said I had to m-marry you——' she'd begun slowly, but now the words were beginning to tumble out '—or you'd destroy Paget's. Well, I couldn't let you do that—I was afraid of what it would do to my father. So James—I mean we——' even now, some vestige of loyalty to James made her determined to share Alex's fury '—thought of a plan.'

Lori glanced at him, but his face, above the white lace frill, was cast into shadow by the wall lights. All she could see was the tautness of his mouth and the hard line of his jaw.

'I was to go through with the marriage, but I was to refuse to s-sleep with you. James—I mean we—thought that that way, you'd come to—to hate me so much that you'd be glad to be rid of me, agree to an annulment, and sell us back Paget's as well.'

She paused, but he might have been made of granite for all the reaction her words had produced. 'I'm sorry, Alex, I really am. It was just that, at the time—well, you really gave us no alternative, did you?' She gave him a hesitant smile, which he completely ignored.

'And is that what you want?' His voice was very remote. 'An annulment—and Paget's, of course.'

'No, it isn't. I thought it was, but no. I told James tonight—I wrote to him last week, but he was here, of course, and didn't get the letter—that I couldn't go through with it.'

'Because you haven't the guts, I suppose.'

'No, not that.' To him, she was every kind of liar and cheat—and now a coward, as well. How could she ever convince him otherwise, for they were separated, not by a few feet of carpet but by a world of anger and mistrust? Oh, please, she thought, let me make him see.

The fingers of one hand were convulsively pleating the fine muslin ruffle at her neckline. She stared down, barely seeing it, but then——

'This dress, Alex.' She looked directly up at him. 'Why do you think I chose it of all others?'

He lifted one shoulder in a negligent half-shrug. 'I have no idea.'

'No one else has ever called me his *Primavera*. I wore it for you.' In spite of herself, her voice shook. She was opening herself out to him, putting herself totally in his power. 'I couldn't *tell* you how I feel, so I showed you.'

'Showed me what?' He was inexorable.

'That I love you.'

The softly spoken words fell into the room and then there was silence, so that all she could hear was her own pounding heart.

Alex did not move a muscle. It had all been for nothing. And suddenly, overwrought as she was, the trauma of the evening burst through her fragile composure. From somewhere very deep inside her a sob was building, forcing its way upwards. She put both hands to her mouth, but it was no use. The sob burst out of her with a tearing sound, followed by another then another, until her slender body shook under the force of them.

Next moment, he had taken her in his arms, cradling her head to his chest, stroking her hair, until at last the sobs subsided. Then he held her away from him and looked down at her with a strange, lop-sided smile.

'You know, *cara*, tears are an unfair weapon.'

'I'm s-sorry.' She gave a sniffle and two more tears rolled down her lashes and hung there, quivering, until Alex gently flicked them away with his little finger.

'Lori?' he said huskily.

'Yes?' She smiled tremulously up at him then, putting her hand up, caressed his cheek, saying in that tender gesture what she couldn't say in words.

Alex seized her hand, pressing his lips to the soft palm, then next moment, as if something inside them both had snapped, they were reaching out to one another, fingers feverishly tearing aside the frail barriers which stood between their naked bodies. There was no finesse, not even any tenderness. Scooping her up into his arms, he dropped her on to the bed, and as she fell she reached up to him, pulling him down to her. He moved across her, nudging her knees apart, as he had done on the night of their wedding, but, this time, every fibre of her on fire for him, she welcomed him joyfully.

Just once he paused, felt the moist warmth which already waited to enfold him, and slid into the length of her. She felt the thrust to her very core and gasped, though less with pain than with the shock of the pleasure, so intense that it was all but unbearable as, deep inside her, he began to move, driving into her again and again with an urgent, pulsating rhythm.

Outside that rhythm, those hands which grasped at sweat-slicked skin, and the rasping breaths which thundered in each other's ears, nothing existed—nothing surely ever had existed. For this was the moment she'd waited for since the very first time she'd met Alex. It was simply that she hadn't realised that this—this terrifying, marvellous, unbearable sensation—was what she'd needed to make her whole.

And then, as her nails bit deep into the flesh of his shoulder, she felt his whole body clench, he half raised himself, withdrawing slightly from her, then, while the universe shivered into atoms around her, with one final, powerful thrust, he collapsed on to her...

Aeons later, Lori struggled up from the deep pit of oblivion into which she'd been hurled. She opened her eyes and saw Alex, all those harsh lines gone from his face, lying on his side, watching her.

'Lori,' he said softly, and laid his hand across her stomach in a tender gesture of possession.

'Y-yes?'

'Nothing. Just—Lori.' And taking her hand, he gently nuzzled the palm. 'Did I hurt you, *amore mio*?' His voice was muffled.

'No—oh, no.' She smiled shyly at him. 'It was *wonderful*.'

He laughed softly. 'Ah, but next time——' He let the promise hang in the air and their eyes met, then she looked down, ashamed that he should see the eagerness, the greed for his body, in her eyes.

'Oh—my dress.' The *Primavera* gown was lying in a tangled heap at the foot of the bed, where Alex had thrown it, and she reached to pick it up. It was ruined— he'd removed her from it simply by ripping apart the zip, tearing the fragile muslin in a dozen places.

'If Signorina Giannini could see it now, whatever would she say?'

'She'd be well pleased with the results of her labours, I should think,' he said, with a wicked grin.

Taking the dress from her, he tossed it on to the floor to join the other clothes that lay scattered across the carpet. Her eyes went slowly from his boots, which she'd helped tug off with feverish hands, to his face, then she coloured slightly, biting at her underlip.

'Don't look like that, *carissima*,' he said quickly. 'Love between man and woman is glorious—the most perfect rapture human beings are capable of.'

'But you'll think I'm——'

'—An abandoned young woman? Of course.' His voice teased her. 'But didn't I tell you once that those fires burned within you? And to discover the truth to-night of all nights.' All at once, he struck his hand to his forehead in a dramatic gesture. '*Cielo*—I almost forgot.'

Going over to his wardrobe, he slid open the door and took out two white-wrapped boxes, which he dropped on to the bed beside her. She picked up the smaller one and, when she opened it, nestling inside was a heavy gold chain, with one perfect pear-shaped emerald hanging from it.

Taking her left hand, he held her engagement ring up to the pendant. 'He told me they'd be a perfect match.' When, too overwhelmed to speak, she looked at him, he went on, 'I didn't know what to get you for your birthday, but then last week the jeweller rang me to say that—by pure chance, of course—this had come his way and he thought I might be interested.'

'It's beautiful, Alex,' she said huskily. As it lay in her palm, the stone flickered intense green fire.

'I should have given it to you earlier, for you to wear at the party, but getting back late I completely forgot. But it isn't morning yet, so—happy birthday, *amore mio*.'

Taking it from her, he put it round her neck and the stone swung gently between her pale, rounded breasts.

'Don't forget this.' He gestured towards the other, much larger box.

'Oh, but you mustn't give me anything else,' she protested.

'But this is your wedding gift.'

And when she undid it and unwrapped the layers of soft tissue she found the loving cup, now finished and polished. She held it up between her hands, seeing how the light shone through it, then Alex leaned across, lightly flicked the edge, and the glass rang softly.

'It's perfect,' she breathed. 'Thank you, Alex.'

'But we must drink from it straight away. Otherwise it's very bad luck.'

Reaching for his black wrap, he shrugged it on and went off, to return a few minutes later carrying an ice bucket and a bottle.

'Lift the cup,' he commanded, and when she obeyed he filled it almost to the brim with foaming pink champagne.

She held it out to him. 'Have some.'

'No—you first. But we must hold it together.'

Each taking a curved handle, they raised the cup and Lori put her lips to it. The icy cold liquid ran down her throat, the bubbles pinpricking at her tonsils.

'Mmmm, wonderful. Now you, Alex.' And he too drank from it before passing it back to her. This time, as she drank, she was conscious of his eyes watching her over the rim, and at his expression she——

'Keep it steady. You're spilling it.'

She looked down, giggling. 'Oh, dear, so I am.'

There was a trail of pale pink bubbles across her right breast, but when she went to mop it up Alex stopped her. 'Let me.'

Lowering his head, he licked up the bubbles, his tongue sliding sensuously over her soft flesh, until she gasped and bit her lip as the need for him stirred inside her again.

He lifted his head for a moment and looked at her, his eyes dark smoky grey with desire, then he lowered it once more, his mouth fastening on her nipple, licking round it, tasting it, teasing it, releasing it then taking it between his teeth again, over and over, until her fingers knotted themselves in his hair and she pressed his head to her. But when his searching mouth moved lower, towards her abdomen, she stopped him.

'Alex.' A breathless sigh.

'Mmmm?'

'Teach me—to make love to you.'

'All in good time.' And his tongue delicately circled her navel until she shuddered violently.

'No—I want to please you.' She said it on a gasp, fighting down her own desire, and gave his head a little tug.

'Very well.' He rolled away from her on to his back and spread his hands, lazy laughter glinting in his eyes. 'I'm all yours, *cara*.'

Slowly, rather shyly, she lifted her hand and circled across his chest, her fingers brushing the fuzz of fine dark hair then moving rhythmically across his nipples until they tensed and sprang up against her skin.

'Do you like that?' she asked softly.

'Could be.' She could hear the laughter in his voice.

Tentatively, she moved lower, tracing intricate spirals across his belly, marvelling as she did so at the flat ridges of muscle beneath the satin skin, then lower, so that her fingertips slid through the soft bush of hair and on to his inner thigh.

'And that?'

'Of course.' But there was no laughter now.

'And—this?' she whispered.

Alex gave a groan. 'You little witch—stop it at once. This time, I want to take the whole night.'

But Lori, feeling a fierce joy surge through her at the knowledge of her power over him, only smiled provocatively through her lashes until, with another groan of surrender, he seized hold of her.

Straight away, they were caught in a whirlwind of passion. It roared round their heads, snatched them up, tossed them around then threw them both down like broken dolls, to lie shattered and spent in each other's arms...

It was dawn when Lori roused, the room filled with that pale translucent light which came only between day and night. Alex lay propped on his elbow, watching her. There were still some half-dried tears on her cheeks from that final cataclysmic upheaval; he lifted one indolent finger and wiped them away.

'Oh, Alex.' Her voice trembled, and he didn't speak, just gave her a funny little smile which made her insides twist painfully, before taking her in his arms.

Now, he made love to her slowly, sensually, his only weapons his hands and mouth, until her blood turned to thick honey in her veins with the intense sweetness coursing through her. She turned her head restlessly to and fro on the pillow, murmuring his name over and over in broken phrases, but when she tried to pull him down to her he held her by the wrists with one hand, the other continuing its assault on her ravished senses.

Time after time, he brought her to the very edge of extinction, but each time, as she moaned for him to take her now—he was killing her—he stifled her protests with his mouth, shushing gently, calming her, drawing her

back from that final brink. And then, as her flesh
trembled and quivered under his touch and she lay
helpless, he would rouse within her once again that slow
erotic spiral with sensations which went beyond pleasure,
or even pain, so that in the end, filled with molten heat,
she became nothing but a bubble of white-hot glass,
being worked to a higher and yet higher pitch of delicacy
in the hands of a master craftsman.

When, at last, Alex did take full possession of her
body, this time with infinite slowness, she felt the soft
pink inner folds of flesh open around him then close,
holding him prisoner. And when he began to move she
clutched him, her eyes fixed and unseeing, then, as her
womb contracted sharply on itself, she called his name
on a long, wild cry. Nothing in this world, she knew—
nothing at all—would ever be quite the same again, for
Alex had broken her into tiny fragments of glass, melted
and remade her, in a totally different form...

Forgive me, *cara*, for not giving myself the pleasure
of seeing you wake. I have some crucial *pâte de verre*
tests arranged for this morning, but I shall be home
early.

Lori skimmed through the note then laid it back on
the bedside table, Alex's bold, black writing still visible,
as a ridiculous little spurt of disappointment ran through
her. Oh, don't be a fool. Of course he had to go. And
he'll be home early—he's made a point of saying that.

She'd get Olga to prepare a special meal...they'd have
a candlelit supper for two out on the balcony over-
looking the canal...she'd wear the blue silk...no—she
caught her breath—that lipstick-red Valentino dress,
which had hung in her wardrobe unworn for weeks...and
then afterwards——

She felt herself blush at the images she was creating, laughed, then pushing back the covers went through to the bathroom. Somehow, she wasn't quite sure how, she ought to be different. She looked in the full-length mirror, and saw that it was true. Although the same Lori gazed back at her, she *had* changed subtly.

There was a glowing bloom on her skin which had not been there before. What had Alex said, as the first rays of sunlight streamed across the bed and she lay drowsily in his arms? 'You have skin like pearls in wine.' And then he'd softly stroked her into sleep.

And her face too. There was a delicate peony flush on her normally pale cheeks, her eyes were soft yet brilliant green, and her lips—they were parted, full and sensual, pouting from Alex's kisses...

When she went downstairs the staff were scurrying around, clearing up after the party. Lori went through to the kitchen. 'Please, let me help,' she begged, but when she tried to put on an apron the housekeeper, horrified at the very idea of *la signora* dirtying her hands, shooed her—very politely—away.

So she retreated, taking with her a tray of coffee, orange juice and hot rolls and butter. The dining-room was in turmoil, so she finally took refuge in Alex's office, where she knew that none of the staff dared set foot.

The desk was littered with photographs and plans of the new house. Last night she'd heard him talking to Emma and Marcello about it—he must have brought them in here to show them. She cleared a space for her tray, poured herself some coffee and began to eat, idly glancing through them.

Very soon, Alex would take her there—and he'd let her help him now. Perhaps she could do the colour schemes... This must be the kitchen, a wood-burning stove in the corner... a lovely sunny peach would go perfectly with those pine units—and maybe some touches of soft green and white... And this would be a bedroom, the ceiling stretching up to the rafters for coolness. How lovely to wake there and look out at the green hills all round...

As she pulled out another photograph from the pile, she saw beneath it a brown manila envelope. Yet more photos, no doubt—how proud Alex was of his new toy. A little smile playing round her lips, she opened it then slid out several sheets of paper, covered in what looked like a series of complex mathematical formulae. The smile turning to a puzzled frown, she turned the papers over, to see yet more equations and, at the top of one, written in Alex's unmistakable hand, '*Pâte de Verre*—temperature ranges.'

Surely, that was what he and Giulia had been working on, trying to develop a new, more reliable production method. But in that case, what were they doing here, lying among his house plans, for any prying eyes to get a glimpse of?

And suddenly she felt certain that this was exactly what had happened last time, four years ago. Alex had been so sure then that those top-secret glass designs were securely locked away—but, instead, he'd left them among the old ones he'd given her as a parting gift. The exultation welled up in her. Even after last night, she could not be sure whether he still thought that she'd stolen them. But now he must surely believe her.

First, though, she had to keep them secure for him. Sliding the papers back into the envelope, she got up and turned to the wall safe. Automatically, she put her hand to the combination dial and, at the same time as she thought, How stupid, you don't know the number, amazingly, the safe door swung open at her touch.

Now that really was careless. Alex just couldn't have known what he was doing last night—or was it, perhaps, this morning? Smiling to herself, she pulled the door wide open to slide the envelope on to the bottom shelf.

'So there you are, *cara.*'

Alex's voice, warm with indulgence, made her leap almost clean through her skin. She spun round.

'Oh—oh, Alex, what a fright you gave me. I thought you were out for the whole day.'

As she laughed with relief, he came slowly across to her.

'What are you doing here, Lori?' Very subtly, his voice had changed.

'It's such a mess everywhere, I brought my breakfast in here. And look, I found this envelope lying among the photographs. Anyone could have taken it.'

'So they could,' he agreed, but she felt a slight prickle of unease at his cool tone, his watchful eyes.

'Anyway, I knew you'd want me to put it away.'

'And how did you open the safe?'

'It was already open. You know, Alex,' she smiled at him, 'I'm sure this is what must have happened when——'

'Do you know what I think, Lori? I think that you were not replacing that envelope, but taking it out.'

'Oh.' The last of the radiance drained from her face, as she clapped a hand to her mouth. He too was very pale, his mouth set.

'Alex,' she began unsteadily. 'You can't still think that I'm a th-thief—not after last night.' Her voice broke.

'Can't I?' His eyes were winter cold, and they froze her to her very heart. 'Let me tell you how I see it, my

sweet. No——' as she tried to interrupt. He did not raise
his voice an iota, but she was silenced. 'I was actually
foolish enough to tell you in my note that I would be
out all day, which would give you all the time you needed.
And I also told you that we were beginning tests on the
new range. So—you panicked. If you were to do anything, it had to be soon.'

'But—why should I? After all,' through the deep hurt
in her, there came a bitter edge to her voice, 'what would
be the point? You own Paget's now.'

His lips curled into a thin line. 'Don't come the
innocent with me. I've fallen for that trick once too often
already.'

He caught hold of her by the elbows, his fingers, which
had so recently roused her to ecstasy, digging cruelly into
her flesh. As she bit back her cry of pain his face twisted
and, as if he dared not trust himself near her, he pushed
her away from him so that she stumbled back hard
against the wall, jarring her shoulder.

'There are plenty of other glass manufacturers besides
Paget's who would give a great deal to get hold of the
fruits of our research.' He paused. 'Maldini, for
instance.'

'No!' She gazed at him, horrified. 'You can't
think——'

'Why not? Last night, when I found you and Forsyth
locked in that loving embrace, my first reaction was the
right one, after all. Before I allowed myself to be persuaded otherwise.' This time, she wasn't sure whether
the contempt was for her or himself.

'You're wrong, Alex, wrong all along the line.
I——'

'You had finalised details for stealing—yes, *stealing*,'
as she flinched from the ugly word, 'the formulae—or

at least for making them available for him to copy. That way, you could have got them safely back—and if I hadn't had my mind on other things this morning,' a humourless smile flickered across his features, 'and had to return for them, I need never have been any the wiser. I really must congratulate you, my sweet. Such an improvement on your rather crude methods of four years ago. Or perhaps we have the more subtle Mr Forsyth to thank.'

'Look, Alex, I don't believe for an instant that James is involved in this. *You* left them here, mixed up with all these photos, you must have done. But when I asked James how he'd got into the party, he did say something about having friends in the right places.'

'Precisely. Who better a friend than my wife, and what better a place than my bed?'

The colour rushed to her face and throat then ebbed again, so that she was colourless once more. She felt like crumpling to the floor at his feet, but somehow she had to defend herself—there was no one else to. 'I said last night that you were determined to think the worst of me, and it's true.'

'What else can I think?'

'You could think that I would never do such a thing.'

'And just why should I do that?'

'Because I love you, and, whatever you say to me, I shall go on loving you.'

Just for an instant, he stared down at her upturned face. But then, almost sadly, he shook his head. 'Oh, no, my sweet innocent—not this time. Last night, like a fool, I allowed myself to be duped by a lovely face, a beautiful dress and——' his voice hardened again with fury at himself '—a few tears. But not now.'

'Oh, you needn't worry, Alex, I shan't shed any more tears. But just tell me this—why would I cheat you?'

'For revenge, of course, my dear little vendetta bride. What else?'

'So—you really believe I would do that to you?' Her heart was coming apart inside her, fracturing into tiny pieces of anguish, so that she could barely get the words out.

He shrugged slightly, as if the question was of no real interest to him. 'You really give me no alternative.'

'But you must let me——'

'Oh, for God's sake, just get out of my house, will you?' Then, as she stared blindly up at him through the sheen of tears, which came in spite of her proud words, 'And get out of my life, for ever!'

CHAPTER TWELVE

SNATCHING up the manila envelope, Alex turned on his heel and went out of the room. Lori heard the housekeeper's voice in the hall, the briefest monosyllable from Alex in reply, then the front door banged behind him.

'Oh, Alex.' The choked words were dragged out of her and she screwed her face up as a shaft of physical pain lanced through her body. She went to sink down into his chair but then, hearing footsteps outside, instead crossed to the window and stood staring out. No one came in, though, but, all the same, she couldn't hide in here all day.

Alex wanted her gone, didn't he? 'Get out of my house... out of my life.' The words were like a funeral bell tolling, and he had killed something inside her, so that she would never be quite whole again. All the same though, she had to pretend, and to make believe that she was still alive. 'Get out of my life'...

At the British Airways departure desk, barely aware of what was going on around her, she joined a straggling queue of English tourists going home. She closed her eyes and felt herself sway slightly. What was she doing leaving Italy, Alex's country, her home now? But he doesn't want you in it, does he? That cold little inner voice was back. Get on the plane—you can be at Mallards tonight.

For a moment, her wounded soul ached for the balm of country peace and tranquillity, the trees rustling, the roses scenting the quiet night air.

'Signora?'

Lori's eyes flew open, to see the smartly uniformed young woman looking questioningly up at her.

'Oh, I'm sorry. I—I've changed my mind,' she blurted out, then, quite unaware of the curious stares, she turned, picked up her case and walked quickly across to the hire-car desk.

This had to be the road. Lori glanced down at the map, provided by the hire firm, and set it in her mind alongside the one in Alex's office. Yes, it was the only road heading west out of the village. She slowed, leaning forward to peer through the windscreen. Over there, all on its own on the hillside, was—surely—a house.

She turned the Fiat off along a narrow track and when this dwindled into grassy ruts she stopped and got out. Beside her was a tall, overgrown hedge and set in it a dilapidated wooden gate. She squeezed through and there it was, exactly as in all those photographs—Alex's house.

Rough whitewashed walls, a fig tree spreading its arching branches over it, the roof brand-new with soft rosy pink tiles, a clump of cypresses behind it and in front a grassy space with a couple of gnarled olive trees, beneath them an old table and bench. Then a small orchard, ripening apples and pears gleaming in the low early evening sun, and beyond that again meadows rolling away down the hillside. So simple, yet so beautiful—and it brought a hard lump to her throat.

She tried the front door but it was locked. Well, of course it's locked, you fool. But to come all this way and not—just once—see inside his house—that was cruel. Maybe the back . . .

But the back door, half hidden by a vine which cascaded across the old pergola and down the walls, was locked as well.

Lori stood for a moment, her hands flat against the wood, but then, as she turned away, she saw that one window was a fraction ajar. Hunting round for a stick, she pushed it through the gap, jiggled the catch—and a moment later it swung open and she scrambled in over the low sill.

She was in the kitchen—just as in the photos. She'd been right—peach *would* look good with these antique-finish pine units, with little touches of willow green... Oh, God, was it only that morning that she'd sat planning long days spent up here with Alex, at his side, helping him? She pressed the back of her hand to her mouth to smother a whimper of pain. Don't think about it. But you have to, Lori. You have to keep thinking about it—reminding yourself of how he looked at you with hatred and contempt. Because that's the only way to cauterise the wound, to sear your pain—and your love—out of you.

Next door to the kitchen was what would one day be an attractive living-room, with wooden beams and freshly whitewashed stone walls. Alongside the new patio window an old padded lounger was pulled up, beside it a pile of paperback books and an empty wine glass.

Upstairs were a bathroom and two bedrooms—a small one and another running the width of the house. She stood in the doorway looking in, feeling a strange reluctance to enter what was clearly where Alex slept when he came to work here.

Over there was a huge window, from floor to rafters, and beside it was a mattress, a couple of pillows and a folded quilt. He obviously lay on this mattress, looking

out at the lights in the valley towards Padua, and upwards to the stars. The old wardrobe in the corner had
swung open—in it she could see casual clothes hanging,
jeans, check shirts and dungarees, and, kicked off into
the bottom, a pair of old black rope-soled espadrilles.

This house was full of Alex—not only the faintest tang
of his aftershave, which seemed to linger in the
bathroom, but his books, his clothes, and downstairs in
the kitchen a couple of simple yet beautifully shaped
glass bowls which she somehow knew he'd made. And
it was full of his life here—a life she would never share.

And all because of his own carelessness and his
stubborn refusal to believe that it just might be possible
that he could make a mistake. How dared he? Without
warning, the righteous anger flared inside her. It was a
dangerous combination with that slight dizziness from
not having eaten all day—enough to make her decide
there and then to go back and have it out with him, to
send her running headlong downstairs to snatch up her
bag, hurl back the bolts on the door, slam it to behind
her and race back to her car.

Only when she'd reversed into the hedge, over-revving
the unfamiliar engine, and was hurtling back down the
winding track, did she realise first that, while she'd been
in the house, dusk had fallen; second that she did not
know where the light switch was; and thirdly that just
around the corner ahead a powerful pair of headlights
was cutting through the failing light.

The car roared towards her, its lights blinding her. Just
at the last moment, the driver must have seen her, for
with a squeal of tyres and brakes he hurled the car hard
to the left and went into a long skid. She felt a violent
shudder as it scraped along the side of her little Fiat
then, as she watched, her heart in her throat, it hurtled

across the verge and came to a halt with a horrible crunching noise, the bonnet and one wing crushed against a tree.

Lori, feeling that at any moment she was going to be very sick, forced herself out and, stumbling across to the other car, she dragged open the driver's door.

And saw Alex. He was just extricating himself from his seat-belt, and at the expression on his face she clapped one hand to her mouth and retreated a few feet.

He climbed out slowly and stood regarding her. He had a graze on one cheek and was extremely pale, but otherwise he seemed to be in one complete, beautiful piece.

'Oh, Alex.' There was a little catch in her voice. 'Are you all right?'

'No thanks to you if I am.' He took a deep, furious breath. 'For God's sake, don't you English use head-lights at night?'

'I—I couldn't find the switch,' she whispered miserably.

'And you were intending to drive all the way to Padua without them, I suppose?' he snarled. 'Probably—it's just the sort of damn fool thing I'd expect from——'

'Just shut up, will you?' They were both yelling at each other now. 'If you hadn't been driving like a maniac you'd have seen me. But of course, *all* Italians drive like maniacs, don't——'

'And you shut up, too. You're the maniac, bombing down here like a bat out of hell—without lights.'

'All right, all right, you've made your point.' The after-shock was getting to her now and she could feel herself starting to tremble. Her eyes strayed to the once so-sleek Alfa Romeo. 'I-is it badly damaged?'

He briefly surveyed the crumpled metal, then said laconically, 'As write-offs go, I suppose it's not too bad.'

'Oh, I'm so s-sorry.' Her mouth drooped.

'For God's sake—do you think I care *that much* about the bloody car?' He took a step towards her then stopped, jamming his hands into his pockets. 'Don't you realise, you little fool, that you could have been killed?'

'Could have got us both killed, you mean. But maybe that would——'

'Would what?'

'Oh, nothing.' Hot tears were pricking her eyes, and she turned her head away. 'Are—are you going up to the house?'

'That was the general idea.'

'I think my car's OK. Shall I give you a lift?'

'I think I'd rather walk—if you don't mind, that is.'

So they walked back up the track in silence, Lori trying to whip up the anger she'd felt only a short while before but only succeeding in feeling unutterably miserable.

He pushed open the gate and stood back to let her through, but then all at once her knees began very slowly buckling under her. As she clutched a hand to her forehead, he put his arm around her waist—very stiffly, though—and half-carried her to the back door.

It was wide open, and when he glanced down at her she muttered, 'I thought I'd shut it. I got in through the window.'

'Ah, I see.'

In the kitchen, still keeping a hold of her, with one foot he hooked a chair away from the table and lowered her into it. Then he lit a big oil-lamp and set it on the window sill. Its golden light made outside very dark, inside very warm and friendly-seeming, and Lori's frozen heart contracted painfully.

'Are you all right?' In the lamplight, his grey eyes gleamed.

'I—I think so.'

'Hmmm.'

Opening a cupboard, he fished out a bottle of cognac and two glasses, poured them each a stiff measure, and dropped into the chair facing her. He cradled the glass between his fingers, swirling the amber fluid and staring moodily down at it.

'Did . . . ?' she began at last, then stopped.

'Yes?' He did not look up.

'Did you know I was here?'

'Of course.' He still did not look up. 'After racing round the airport, the railway station and the ferry port, I tried the car-hire firms, and there can't be many young women with British driving licences in the name of Lorina Jane Paget asking for maps of Padua and district.'

'I see.' One part of her was filled with a bitter joy, the other part with anguish. 'But, Alex—there was no point—in your coming after me, I mean.' She spoke very softly, her head bent so that her silky hair fell forward around her face. 'Thinking what you do of me, surely it's best that we don't ever see each other again?'

'Lori.' The sudden tenderness in his voice made her head jerk up, and before she could move back he took her hand. 'I had to come, because I have—something to tell you.' There was a constraint, almost a diffidence in his voice that she'd never heard before. 'You see, I know that you are innocent—and that you were innocent four years ago.'

'Oh.' She gave a gasp as pure happiness flooded through her. 'But—how?'

He grimaced. 'I hadn't even reached Murano this morning before it hit me that I had to be wrong. How could I have loved you last night, had you lie in my arms, and not know if I was holding a liar and a cheat?'

'But this morning you thought I was just up to my old thieving tricks again.'

'I tried telling myself that, yes,' he said sombrely. 'You know, Lori, when I found you with those papers, I think a part of me actually wanted you to be guilty.'

'But why?'

'Because if you weren't, it would have meant that I was wrong four years ago as well, and the great Alex Baresi must never be wrong.'

He got up abruptly and crossed to the window, staring out into the darkness, shoulders hunched. 'So that's why I came back to the house again—and found the real thief in my office, trying to complete her unfinished business from the night before.'

'The real thief?'

'Yes—Giulia.' He swung round towards her. 'As soon as I saw her face, I knew, and suddenly everything clicked into place. She was the only one to know the combinations of the two safes—that one and the one at Murano, four years ago—and to have worked with me on both projects. Anyway, I confronted her with it and she—well——' he seemed to recoil from some appalling memory '—she tried denying it at first, but then something broke in her, and all the poison came pouring out. She's hated you, Lori, since the first time you came here.'

'She's—hated me? But I—I thought she liked me.' Her voice shook. 'She was my friend.'

'Oh, *cara*.' Again, Alex took a step towards her, and again seemed to rein himself back. 'She took those designs four years ago and deliberately hid them among the others, banking on your being blamed.'

'And she did the same this time?'

'Well, not exactly.' He paused. 'I'm sorry, Lori, but what I'm going to tell you will hurt you deeply. Her boyfriend—the one I teased her about—well, he turns out to be Forsyth.'

'James?'

'Remember what he said—about having friends in the right places? Oh, *carina*, I knew it would grieve you, but you have to know. She met him in Venice—I imagine he manoeuvred it, although she doesn't realise that. Her invitation to your party included a partner, and she saw it as the perfect opportunity to take the formulae for him to pass on to his new employers.'

'Maldini?'

'Precisely.' His features hardened for a moment. 'She was disturbed in the middle of removing the papers, hid them among the photos; I sent Forsyth packing——' a grim smile of reminiscence '—so she was forced to return for them this morning—only to come face to face with me.'

'But why?' The pain at Giulia's treachery was tiny in comparison with the anguish she'd suffered already, yet it still hurt dreadfully.

'Why did she try to hurt you, you mean? I've told you—because she hates you.'

'Yes, but why? W-what did I ever do to her?' Lori's voice wobbled dangerously.

'I'm afraid——' Alex spoke as if he had no stomach for the words '—it's because she loves me. Apparently, she's always loved me.'

'Oh, no. And you had no idea?'

'None.'

'Poor Giulia.' Lori's eyes filled with tears. It was so easy to see how she could have fallen for a man like Alex, and to have had to endure years of unspoken, unrequited love...

'It all came pouring out—about how she's always fantasised about me coming to her eventually. But then, when I married you—well, all her hopes were finally dashed.'

'And she threw in her lot with James,' Lori said slowly. 'But four years ago—why then?'

'Because, my sweet, somehow she saw then what no one else saw, that even I was too blind to see.'

'What was that?' A wild, yet utterly impossible hope was rising in her.

'When you went back to England, I told myself a thousand times that I was crazy. I, a sophisticated man of the world, who could have my pick of poised, beautiful women, to be haunted by a gauche seventeen-year-old, an unformed schoolgirl. I even hung a painting in my room simply because it reminded me of her. So— just like today, I was actually glad to convince myself that you were a thief.'

'It doesn't matter, Alex,' she put in softly, but he didn't seem to hear.

'But it was no use. I arrived at Paget's that day, and into the office came that young girl, transformed into a slender, wayward nymph with a tender mouth and flashing sea-green eyes.' He pulled a wry face. 'And, at that precise moment, Alex Baresi was lost for ever.'

'So—you didn't marry me out of revenge?' she asked hesitantly.

'Of course not.' In his grey eyes there was a flash of the old, familiar Alex. 'I simply took one look at that Forsyth and decided that, come hell or high water, nothing would give me greater pleasure than to peel you away from his cold clutches.'

'I see.' Her thumbnail was going round and round a tiny whorl in the pine table.

'Oh, *carissima*, don't look like that. Of course that's not why.'

'Why, then? I know you don't love me, but——'

'Don't love you?' He stared down at her in blank astonishment—and fury. 'What the hell do you mean, I don't love you? Haven't you been listening? Of course I love you, you idiot. I worship every inch of you, from that beautiful hair down to those——' he gave her a lop-sided smile '—ten delectable dusty toes.'

'Oh, Alex.' The joy was flooding through her now, thawing her frozen heart. 'But why didn't you tell me?'

'Tell a woman who never lost an opportunity to inform me that she hated and detested the very sight of me—and loved another man into the bargain?' He shook his head ruefully. 'I don't think my pride would have allowed me to do that. And now——' his mouth tightened '—it's too late.'

'Too late?'

'After the abominable way I've treated you, the unforgivable things I've said to you, you can never——' He broke off.

'Forgive you, Alex? But of course I can.' She gave him a tremulous smile. 'You see, I love you.'

'Oh, *amore mio*.' In two strides he had reached her, snatched her up out of the chair and was crushing her to him.

'And Giulia?' Her voice was smothered in his chest. 'Please don't hurt her.'

'Don't worry. I rang my mother, and apparently she was last seen racing out of the villa, screaming that she

was off to join her lover—and they *are* lovers, Lori—
that's another thing she told me. I think they'll be well
suited, don't you?'

'I suppose so,' she murmured. 'Poor Giulia.'

'Or, some might say, poor James. Although maybe
they'll make each other happy.' He paused, gently
rubbing his chin against her hair, then went on reflec-
tively, 'Of course, with Giulia gone I shall need a tal-
ented new designer. You don't happen to know of
anyone, do you?'

'Oh, Alex!' It was surely impossible to contain such
happiness—her heart would burst. 'You know what you
were saying about setting me up to make those glass earrings? Well, I was thinking——'

'Not now, *tesoro*,' he said gently and, holding her away
from him, he bent his head to silence her with a kiss.
'Tell me tomorrow.'

Taking the lamp, he lit their way upstairs. He set it
down on the landing and led her into the big bedroom,
and there, caught between the pale gold of the lamplight
and the pale silver of a full moon, he slowly unbuttoned
her dress and slid it off her, followed by her bra and
panties. Then, as she stood before him, one hand to her
breast, he loosed her hair and, running his fingers
through it, brought it cascading down to her slender
shoulders.

'My *Primavera*,' he said huskily, and at the expression
on his face—tender yet infinitely sensual—Lori's breath
caught in her throat.

Lifting her into his arms, he laid her down on the
mattress. At their feet were the twinkling lights of the
valley, above their heads a million stars, and in their
hearts perfect, everlasting love.

POSTCARDS FROM EUROPE*

HARLEQUIN PRESENTS*

Hi!

I can't believe that I'm living on Cyprus— home of Aphrodite, the legendary goddess of love—or that I'm suddenly the owner of a five-star hotel.

Nikolaos Konstantin obviously can't quite believe any of it, either!

Love, Emily

Travel across Europe in 1994 with Harlequin Presents. Collect a new Postcards From Europe title each month!

Don't miss
THE TOUCH OF APHRODITE
by Joanna Mansell
Harlequin Presents #1684

Available in September, wherever Harlequin Presents books are sold.

MILLION DOLLAR SWEEPSTAKES (III)

No purchase necessary. To enter, follow the directions published. Method of entry may vary. For eligibility, entries must be received no later than March 31, 1996. No liability is assumed for printing errors, lost, late or misdirected entries. Odds of winning are determined by the number of eligible entries distributed and received. Prizewinners will be determined no later than June 30, 1996.

Sweepstakes open to residents of the U.S. (except Puerto Rico), Canada, Europe and Taiwan who are 18 years of age or older. All applicable laws and regulations apply. Sweepstakes offer void wherever prohibited by law. Values of all prizes are in U.S. currency. This sweepstakes is presented by Torstar Corp., its subsidiaries and affiliates, in conjunction with book, merchandise and/or product offerings. For a copy of the Official Rules send a self-addressed, stamped envelope (WA residents need not affix return postage) to: MILLION DOLLAR SWEEPSTAKES (III) Rules, P.O. Box 4573, Blair, NE 68009, USA.

EXTRA BONUS PRIZE DRAWING

No purchase necessary. The Extra Bonus Prize will be awarded in a random drawing to be conducted no later than 5/30/96 from among all entries received. To qualify, entries must be received by 3/31/96 and comply with published directions. Drawing open to residents of the U.S. (except Puerto Rico), Canada, Europe and Taiwan who are 18 years of age or older. All applicable laws and regulations apply; offer void wherever prohibited by law. Odds of winning are dependent upon number of eligibile entries received. Prize is valued in U.S. currency. The offer is presented by Torstar Corp., its subsidiaries and affiliates in conjunction with book, merchandise and/or product offering. For a copy of the Official Rules governing this sweepstakes, send a self-addressed, stamped envelope (WA residents need not affix return postage) to: Extra Bonus Prize Drawing Rules, P.O. Box 4590, Blair, NE 68009, USA.

SWP-H894

HARLEQUIN®

PRESENTS *plus*

Nathan Parnell needs a wife and mother for his young son. Sasha Redford and her daughter need a home. It's a match made in heaven, although no one's discussed the small matter of love.

Emily Musgrave and her nephew are on the run. But has she compounded her problems by accepting the help of Sandy McPherson, a total stranger?

Fall in love with Nathan and Sandy—Sasha and Emily do!

Watch for

In Need of a Wife by Emma Darcy
Harlequin Presents Plus #1679

and

Catch Me If You Can by Anne McAllister
Harlequin Presents Plus #1680

Harlequin Presents Plus
The best has just gotten better!

Available in September wherever Harlequin books are sold.

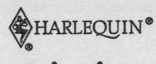

HARLEQUIN®

Weddings, Inc.

THE WEDDING GAMBLE
Muriel Jensen

Eternity, Massachusetts, was America's wedding town. Paul Bertrand knew this better than anyone—he never should have gotten soused at his friend's rowdy bachelor party. Next morning when he woke up, he found he'd somehow managed to say "I do"—to the woman he'd once jilted! And Christina Bowman had helped launch so many honeymoons, she knew just what to do on theirs!

THE WEDDING GAMBLE, available in September from American Romance, is the fourth book in Harlequin's new cross-line series, **WEDDINGS, INC.**

Be sure to look for the fifth book, **THE VENGEFUL GROOM,** by Sara Wood (Harlequin Presents #1692), coming in October.

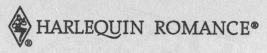

HARLEQUIN ROMANCE®

brings you

Stories that celebrate love, families and children!

Watch for our next Kids & Kisses title in September.

The Dinosaur Lady
by Anne Marie Duquette
Harlequin Romance #3328

A Romance that will move you and thrill you! By the author of
Rescued by Love, On the Line and Neptune's Bride.

Noelle Forrest is "the Dinosaur Lady." Jason
Reilly is the eleven-year-old boy who brings her
a dinosaur fossil that may be her biggest career
break ever—a fossil he found on Matt Caldwell's
ranch.

Noelle discovers that there's room in her life and
heart for more than just her career. There's room
for Jason, who hasn't got a real family of his
own—and for Matt, a strong compassionate man
who thinks children are more important than
dinosaurs....

Available wherever Harlequin books are sold.

Fifty red-blooded, white-hot, true-blue hunks
from every State in the Union!

Look for MEN MADE IN AMERICA! Written by some of
our most popular authors, these stories feature fifty of
the strongest, sexiest men, each from a different state in
the union!

Two titles available every month at your favorite retail
outlet.

In August, look for:

PROS AND CONS by Bethany Campbell
(Massachusetts)
TO TAME A WOLF by Anne McAllister (Michigan)

In September, look for:

WINTER LADY by Janet Joyce (Minnesota)
AFTER THE STORM by Rebecca Flanders (Mississippi)

You won't be able to resist MEN MADE IN AMERICA!
